T0128212

# THE BOUNTY HUNTERS RETURN

JOEY HOFFMAN

Order this book online at www.trafford.com
or email orders@trafford.com

Most Trafford titles are also available at major online book retailers.

Print information available on the last page.

ISBN: 978-1-6987-0148-6 (sc)
ISBN: 978-1-6987-0150-9 (hc)
ISBN: 978-1-6987-0149-3 (e)

Library of Congress Control Number: 2020939122

*Trafford rev. 05/29/2020*

 www.trafford.com

**North America & international**
toll-free: 1 888 232 4444 (USA & Canada)
fax: 812 355 4082

# CONTENTS

Chapter 1    Tunnel Vision ........................................................... 1

Chapter 2    Trouble for Travis ................................................. 13

Chapter 3    The New Guy .......................................................... 19

Chapter 4    A Great Find........................................................... 27

Chapter 5    Her Mother's Threat ............................................ 37

Chapter 6    Stairs to Nowhere ................................................ 45

Chapter 7    A Wish in Time ..................................................... 55

Chapter 8    Out Back................................................................. 67

Chapter 9    Locked Away .......................................................... 75

Chapter 10   A New Direction.................................................... 83

Chapter 11   In The Cemetery .................................................. 95

Chapter 12   A Second Contact............................................... 103

Chapter 13   Assault with A Deadly Weapon......................... 113

Chapter 14   Up on The Skid Trail ......................................... 121

Chapter 15   Taking A Risk...................................................... 131

Chapter 16   Magic Moments................................................... 143

Chapter 17   Race Day .............................................................. 153

Chapter 18   Slipping Out ........................................................ 163

Chapter 19   Letting Go ........................................................... 175

Chapter 20   Bank Robbery...................................................... 187

Chapter 21   The Barbecue ...................................................... 205

# Tunnel Vision

The warrant landed on his desk with urgency. It was now the number one priority for the Underdog's bounty hunting team to catch this fugitive.

William Hoffman opened the surprisingly thin file and began to read aloud the facts to the crew. "His name is James Lolly. He's five feet seven, weighs two hundred and thirty pounds."

"It's mostly in his gut," Swade, the bail bondsman added to the conversation.

Travis wrote the details of the fugitive upon the marker board next to his mugshot. "What else you got?" he turned and asked the boss.

"He doesn't have much of a rap sheet. A few drunk and disorderly charges, second degree assault from 2005, and possession of a stolen gun. He had marijuana on him at the time of his arrest."

"Is that his current charge – the stolen gun?"

Swade nodded. "A twenty thousand dollar bond and this guy decides not to go to court. I called his number, but he isn't answering."

"Is this guy mental or on drugs?" one agent asked.

"I have no reports of any."

"The best place to start would be his place of residence," William continued, "It says here he runs the Reo Hotel here in Kellogg."

"Sounds like he'll be an easy catch!" Travis presumed and they all agreed.

Nathan was excited to be on the Underdog's bounty hunting team. He had recently completed his training, been on plenty of bounties, and now he proudly wore his badge and chain about his neck. He outfitted himself with a bullet proof vest, handcuffs, and pepper spray. He didn't care much to carry a pistol like Travis or William even though he knew how to shoot one.

The five man crew headed out of the office. William, Travis, and Nathan climbed into one vehicle while Swade and Nick followed in the other suv as they started out for the Reo.

The package she had been waiting for had finally arrived snail mail. Dominique was in a state of bliss as she held her newly released novel in her hands. Now in print after two and a half years of writing and editing, she fixed a copy of the novel into a shadow box and added it to her collection atop of her shelf in the living room.

Ian walked into the room playing his portable video game system. He glanced up at his mom who was standing idle, as though she was waiting for him to notice. She wore a proud smile and was pointing a finger at her paperback treasures. "'That's awesome Mom! Now you have three books."

For the rest of the morning, Dominique sat or laid on the couch and gazed over at her fictional work of art. She recalled a bible verse that says a man or woman can rejoice in his labor so she kept grinning. She had many other thoughts going through her head. Ideas for her fourth book and where she would schedule her book signings. She reflected on the memory of her dad who had passed away before she started to pen her first book; how amazed he would feel since he himself never learned to read or write very well.

Nick was dropped off on Mckinley Avenue at the front entrance of the small hotel to keep watch while the rest of the team drove around the block. William maneuvered his vehicle in between two brick buildings and accelerated down the paved alleyway. He stopped at the forepart of a scant parking lot, blocking in some of the tenant's cars.

Swade drove past the entrance of the alley and around a large abandoned building, then turned right and parked in the lot alongside a row of trees. He was facing the hotel so he could notify his comrades over the radio if he spotted James.

William scanned for James' black truck and saw it parked within the nearby shrubs and grass before he and his two rookies jumped out of the suv. Nathan stayed close to the side of the building near the back door while he and Travis noticed the NO VACANCY sign and hastened to the little oval house that was attached to the hotel. They read the word OFFICE on what seemed to be the residential door to James' place. William knocked. They heard the barking of a dog. "James?" he yelled, then knocked again.

The white door came open. A middle aged woman who already bore gray hair appeared. She was puffing on a cigar.

"We're lookin' for James Lolly. Is he here?"

"No," she replied after noticing their garb.

"You must be his wife Linda?"

She nodded.

"When do you expect him back?"

"I don't know. He went to Texas."

"You sure about that? His truck is right there." William pointed at the old jalopy.

"He left with a friend."

"Can we come in and search just to make sure?"

"If he was here, I'd hand his ass over to you myself, but if it helps you to feel better, come ahead." She stepped aside and let them enter.

William and Travis searched the small two bedroom enclosure and found it to be clear. They returned to the outdoors where Linda was waiting. William stared at her. "You need to help us bring James in."

"Like I said, he went to Texas. He needed to get away for a while so he left."

"Were you two arguing?" he asked.

"Sort of."

William increased his tone. "Do you realize what your husband put up for collateral? If James isn't brought in, his bail bondsman will start the process of repo-ing your car."

"My car? That fat man told me he put up his two trucks." She looked away as she frowned with serious thought. "I'll make a call to see if he'll pick up." She went into her oval top shaped house.

"I'll be waiting." William and Travis turned and walked to the gate. "Perhaps that will put a fire under her butt." He sent a friendly wink to the agent.

"You're a sly one." Travis grinned back at him knowing he lied about the car.

The two agents decided to step several feet from the odd shaped house to join forces with Nathan. William looked around and considered all the hiding places James could be in. He radioed to Swade and Nick to hold their positions, then he spotted a tenant exiting from the rear door of the hotel. He stepped to the man. "Excuse me sir. We're looking for James. Have you seen him around?"

"I saw him early this morning. He was walking his dog."

After the tenant walked off, William cast his eyes to Travis and Nathan. "He didn't go to Texas." He lifted his hand and pointed his finger downward. "He's here somewhere. I can feel it!"

"Let's go knock on every door in this freakin' hotel until we find him!" Travis urged.

"I'm in," Nathan remarked.

The three bounty hunters advanced to the rear door of the hotel and entered in. Inside was a lobby and a large staircase that led down to the front of the building where Nick kept guard. They walked past a love seat, a desk with an outdated computer atop of it, and several tall plants.

They knocked on eleven doors with only three answering. With no results of finding their fugitive, they returned through the exit door of the building to the back porch. William scattered his vision about the porch seeing a basement door. He stepped to it and read WATCH YOUR STEP on the small strip. He pondered on the possibility of James being down under so he turned the knob and found it to be locked. He sent Nathan to fetch the crowbar out of the suv as well as the flashlights.

William didn't have to yank hard to get the door to open. He led the way down the wooden staircase into a small room. There was a hall leading to five different doors in which the two rookies checked on while William investigated a singular door separate from the others. He pulled the movable structure forward and after peeking in, he found it to be the back door of a bygone nightclub. The room spoke of dullness and quiet, yet he still tossed the beam from his flashlight about the enclosure, then he closed the door.

William backtracked to the staircase where he descended a second set of steps to yet another door. He called his agents to follow, then after he opened the door, he heard a noise. "Did you hear that?" he turned and asked Travis and Nathan.

"It sounded like a rock falling."

Travis advanced first into the dark enclosure. "It's musty in here." He again breathed in the stale air as he stepped onto the dirt ground and loose pebbles. He shined his light upon a large inoperative boiler. "October 1921," he read the date from the hatch. "Wow!"

Nathan aimed his light opposite of the boiler. "Look at that pile of dirt. It looks like there could be a dead body buried underneath there."

All three agents cast their lights around, observing the ceiling, seeing the water and sewage pipes that ran in through two large gaps in the wall.

William stepped up to one of the openings and shined his light within. "James?" he called out while he spied for markings on the dirt.

Travis informed them of one more door. A door that screamed haunted as he stood in front of it. "I wonder where this one leads to?"

"Let's find out." William moved to join Travis and when he grabbed the knob, he heard footsteps coming from behind him. He turned himself toward the staircase.

"You can't be down here!" Linda warned rather loudly with her tenor voice, "This is private property."

"Did you get a hold of James?"

"No," she shot back, "And if you don't leave now, I'm calling the cops!"

"Wait! Wait a minute." He stopped and watched her stomp up the stairwell, then he radioed to Swade informing him of Linda's intention. He suggested he go and talk to her rather promptly to stall for more time while he and his young help search for their fugitive. He turned and faced the eerie wooden door and pulled it open.

The agents beheld what was on the other side of the door. Horizontal boards were stacked and nailed against the frame up past the knob whereas concrete slabs were piled a bit higher on the other side of that.

Travis stood on his toes and aimed his light beyond the rocks through the scant opening. "I think it's a tunnel. You think James could fit through this passage?"

William considered the layout. "I suppose he could fit. He'd have to stick his feet in between these boards and use them like a ladder to climb over." He inserted his foot into the bottom rift and heaved himself up. He then crawled atop of the pile of slab, stopped and shined his flashlight into the distance. "It is a tunnel! Just the doorway is blocked," he confirmed when he told his two men to follow him.

After the agents conquered the blockade, they stood idle, sending forth the glow from their portable lights as they took in the feel of the rugged tunnel walls.

Nathan studied the dirt ground. "Footprints!"

William cast his light to the ground. "Yea, but who knows how old or new they really are?" He stepped forward as he led the way through some spider webs and soon, they came to a fork. "I'll go this way and you two go that way."

"What if we get lost?" one asked.

"You can't get lost. McKinley Avenue is right above us."

Just then, they felt a weak vibration accompanied by the slight sound of a vehicle passing above.

"I can taste dirt now." Travis smacked his lips as he moved his tongue around.

William made an arrow in the dirt with his shoe for the agents to know where home base is, then he headed west.

Travis and Nathan went the opposite way at a slow pace. "This is kind of creepy." There was silence as they stepped further through the dark, narrow passageway. "I'd better not get bit by a spider," Travis remarked because his brother knew he loathed them.

Nathan chuckled. "Spiders are little. There's nothing to be afraid of. You could just squash em."

While they advanced, they gave ear to any noise or movement and soon they came upon an outlet with slab filled in up to the top. "Must be another door back there leading to a different... something." They turned and continued on.

"MMMMMmmmmmmmm....."

They froze. "Did you hear that?" Travis' eyes grew wide as he tried to look at his brother through the darkness.

"I think it was the ground shifting."

"It sounded like a moan to me."

Their hearts thumped with both excitement and fear as they moved their light beams around the area and listened for the strange utterance to sound again, but it didn't.

"I think these tunnels are haunted."

"Naa.."

The bounty hunters came to another branch in the tunnel. They paused and studied both passageways as they considered which way to go.

"I see a light!" one said.

They stepped to the glow and looked upward to see a small hole in the ground. "I can see a glimpse of the sky."

"I wonder how far we are from Nick?"

"It doesn't matter. We need to keep moving."

More dust gravitated from above with the passing of additional traffic. They backtracked to the original tunnel and continued going east. Within the range of the flashlights' radiance, a black shadow dashed across their path.

"Did you see that?" Nathan's heart began to beat faster.

"Yes I did. James?" Travis called out.

The two men hustled in the direction of the image and immediately came to a dead stop. They moved their flashlights about and observed there to be no space above the slabs for anyone to climb over and escape.

"No way! Where did he go?" Nathan glanced at his brother, then returned to examining the tunnel's features.

"It wasn't James."

"Then who was it?"

Travis hesitated to answer. "A ghost."

"Cool! I hope it comes back." He placed his hand to one side of his mouth and called out, "Hey ghost?"

"What are you doing?" Travis demanded.

"It won't hurt us. We're saved and we have the Holy Spirit living within us that protects us."

"I know that, but I'm not a ghost hunter," he sported, "I'm a bounty hunter."

William came to a dead end soon after leaving Travis and Nathan. He approached and climbed over pile of rocks that was stacked above two feet, then he noted a rickety old ladder which led to an overhead trap door. He radioed to Travis and Nathan for their action report and location, then instructed them to come his way, however, he didn't wait for them to arrive before he stepped cautiously up the aged ladder and push up on the wooden door.

The door creaked slightly when he pressed up on it. He held the structure ajar with the top of his head as he peeked through the gap. He found himself to be underneath a building. The room was dim, vacant of people and furnishings, and it smelled from age. He pushed up on the edge of the trap door until it rested onto the wall, then he climbed up onto the dusty floor.

Leaving the trap door open, William stepped into the large room and moved his flashlight about. He saw small piles of boards lying here and there as well as a few bricks. He observed what was once three or four bowling lanes. "I'm in the old ymca building."

When he directed himself toward the staircase, he heard his two agents ascending the ladder so he turned and walked to them.

Travis stepped out onto the dusty hardwood floor.

"You look pale?" he asked him.

Nathan popped his head up from the trap door entry. "Those tunnels are haunted!" he asserted.

William chuckled as he noticed Nathan's smile. "Did you see a ghost?" He returned his focus onto his sensitive agent.

Travis knew William was teasing him. "I'll be fine," he replied, "It's just the air and dust down there."

"Good. Let's get back to why we're here and tear this place up until we find our man." William closed the trap door, then gestured to the agents to head up to the top floor. "Flush him out and I'll wait down here."

Travis carried his pistol in front of him as he led the way up both sets of stairs. They explored the third floor, circling around unconnected walls, checking every nook and cranny.

Nathan advanced to the anterior side of the building and looked out a window that wasn't boarded up. He cast his sights downward and saw his older brother Nick standing guard. He moved the mike from his radio to his mouth and spoke. "Hey Nick?"

Nick spied the door of the hotel.

Nathan chuckled as he kept his eye on him. "Look up – across the street."

Travis stepped in beside his brother. "Come on.. quit screwing around."

The two agents walked to the staircase and descended to the second floor.

William roamed about the basement, waiting for results from his co-workers when he heard a muffled sneeze. Wondering exactly where it came from, he froze in place to listen. Within ten seconds, he heard the sneeze again, then hurried with light steps to the back end of the basement. He moved his flashlight around the room, but saw only two or three very large pieces of plywood laying across the span of the abandoned swimming pool. He wondered if the pool was filled in with anything or if it was empty. He tiptoed at a slow pace toward the handrail, shining his light from the boards to the concrete trim. When he came to the metal rails and examined them closely, he observed smudged prints amongst the dust. He heard another suppressed sneeze.

Travis and Nathan entered quietly into William's view with a shrug of the shoulders.

William saw their gestures then signaled for them to get ready. He pointed his finger downward at the loose boards. He set his flashlight down and while the two young bounty hunters aimed their light beams upon the entry of the pool, he lifted one of the large boards up past his head.

Nathan stepped in and held it for him.

He knelt and as he shined his light within the enclosure, he observed half the pool to be filled with wood and the other half, he found his prize. James was sitting on a comfortable chair in the dark with his lantern unlit in the corner.

"It doesn't get any sweeter then this!" William boasted. "Why didn't you go to court?" he hollered while he kept the light on him.

James stood and advanced toward the ladder. "I just forgot," he told him.

The agents had James Lolly handcuffed in the front and after a visual search of his hideout, they escorted him to the trap door and down through the tunnels back to the Reo.

As they were emerging from the hotel basement, Swade transmitted over the radio to the team that the cops were present.

"Tell them to go home. We have our fugitive!" William shot back.

# Trouble for Travis

Feeling responsible for their arrests, William apologized to Travis and Nathan, promising to pay their court fines.

"I still can't believe they took us in for trespassing," one of the agents spoke while they walked away from the Wallace jail toward their ride home.

"Only because the hotel's basement wasn't actually James' place of residence," William remarked with contempt.

Dominique met with a rental agent and handed her a check for the lease of a beach house for the up and coming weekend. She had the key and after the realtor left, she again toured the luxurious house then went outside and walked the pathway down to the boat dock. While she stood alone, she beheld the early sunset, then turned aside, eyeing the secluded sandy beach and the large boulders that aligned the shore. She watched two boats as they roared across the lake to their final destinations of the day.

Dominique pondered some moments before she looked down at her left hand and saw the ring indent she still carried on her marriage finger. She welcomed the new gladness within her heart of being apart from Matt. Her divorce was now final and Matt had sold his half of the Underdogs Bounty Hunting business to William and moved out of state.

Travis answered his cell phone as he sat on his couch watching tv.

"Where have you been?" Hannah swiftly demanded of him.

"I've been in jail."

"For two days?" she snapped, "You're a bounty hunter. You should have bonded out right away?"

"I had to wait and go to court just like everyone else. I was also doing other things after I got out," he replied gently in spite of her attitude.

"Oh, sorry," she paused. "Are you gonna come over and see me?"

"Now?"

"Yea. My mom is at work."

"Okay my girl. I'll be there soon."

"Don't forget to park down the street," she cautioned.

Some fifty minutes later, Travis arrived in Hayden at his girlfriend's place. As he walked the block to her house, he carried in his palm, a flowery pattern barrette. Before he could knock on the front door, Hannah had it open.

"You left this at my apartment," he said, then handed the trendy clip to her.

She took the piece and slid it into the thickness of her hair as she kept her eyes focused in on Travis. She pulled him by the arm into the house and kissed him. "I'm glad you came. I have to tell you something."

"Tell me what?" he questioned between kisses.

"Don't be alarmed... but I'm pregnant."

Startled by her statement, he backed away. "Wow. I wasn't expecting you to say that."

"Is this a bad thing?"

Travis hesitated. "Not bad, just kind of early. We've only known each other for two months."

She looked into his vague blue eyes. "You don't want me to be pregnant – do you?"

"We'll deal with it." He observed the sadness in her face. "Come here." He wrapped his thin, yet muscular arms around her, trying to soothe her spirit.

She accepted his embrace and soon she looked upward into his eyes. "Come to my bedroom." She locked the anterior door to the house and led Travis through the short hallway. They entered her room and sat on the bed; Hannah perched herself up on her knees behind him and placed her hands atop of his shoulders and began to rub. She put her mouth close in to his ear. "We do love each other, right?" She took in the enjoyable scent of his cologne.

"Yea, of course." He moaned with delight.

"Well.. you have a good job and by the time the baby is born, I'll be graduated from high school." She hinted of marriage, however, she would wait for him to speak of it.

Travis' mind went a different route. "Does your mom know you're pregnant?" he asked.

"No! She doesn't even know about you."

"Why not? Aren't you allowed to have a boyfriend?"

Before she could answer, they heard from the opposite end of the house, the garage door opening. "My mom's here!" Hannah jumped off the bed to her feet and cast her attention to Travis. "You have to hide!" She guided him toward her closet with force.

"Why? Just tell her now about me."

"I can't."

"Yes you can."

"I'll find out why she's here. Please hide."

He saw the panic in her eyes and stepped backwards into the closet. "You make me feel like a fugitive!" he remarked.

"What?" She rolled the doors to a silent close, ignoring his statement. Hannah stepped out of her bedroom and walked out to the living room. She saw her mother approaching. "I thought you were working the late shift today?"

Kelly set her keys on the counter. "I am. I just have a personal emergency." She headed toward the hallway. "What's that nice smell – new potpourri?"

She didn't answer, rather she watched her mom take a glance in her bedroom as she passed by the gap of the doorway, then enter into her own bedroom.

Hannah crept down the hallway and closed her bedroom door. She returned quickly to the living room where she flipped the switch to turn on the overhead fan.

Five minutes later, Officer Kelly emerged from her bedroom. The radio she wore about her waist sounded of police talk as she stepped through the living room.

"Staying busy today?" Hannah asked her mother.

"No. There's not too much going on right now, but that can easily change. What about you? Are you staying busy?" She expressed concern.

"Of course. I'm getting ready to do my homework."

Kelly took hold of her keys from the counter and headed through the kitchen toward the garage door.

"Bye Mom."

"Get rid of that funny smell!" she shot back.

Hannah waited for her mom to drive away before rushing to the bedroom to let Travis know it was okay to come out of the closet. "Sorry about that Babe," she spoke.

He glared at her as he stepped out. "You seriously need to tell your mom about me. I'm not hiding anymore." He observed the hesitant expression upon her young face, then looked into her unpredictable eyes. "You make me think you've got a secret?" he probed with a raise of his brow.

"No." she innocently proclaimed.

"Then why haven't you told her about me?"

"She'll get into our business!"

"I have an odd feeling about something." He kissed her on the lips, then turned. "I'll see you later."

"Wait!" she begged, "Don't leave yet." She followed him out of her bedroom and through the hallway. "When will I see you next?"

Travis stopped and turned to face her. "You're mom is spooky Hannah."

She quickly withdrew her shirt and bra upward to her chin, letting her breasts go bare for him to view.

"Mmm.. You're making it hard for me to leave," he responded in a lower tone as he reached forward to caress her nipples.

"Then stay."

The sun began to rest behind the western mountains when Travis accelerated from alongside the curb, then cruised the side street to the main highway. He drove a mile before he noticed flashing blue and red lights coming up behind him. "What the hell? I didn't do anything wrong!" He slowed his truck over to the side of the road. After parking, he waited and watched through his side mirror as the officer approached. He rolled the window down.

"License, registration, and proof of insurance," she spoke firmly.

"Why'd you pull me over?" he growled.

"Speeding."

"Speeding? How fast was I going?"

"Thirty-seven."

He wore a confused look upon his face. "The speed limit is only thirty-five."

"It's still speeding," the officer replied.

He gathered the requested information, then handed the assortment of paperwork to the officer who now had her face down to his window. She used her nose to investigate the air that came from within his cab. "You wear a ton of cologne. I could smell you the moment I stepped into my house!"

Travis swallowed hard.

"Aren't you going to say anything?" She tried to provoke him, however, he remained silent. "I'll be right back." She took a step backwards and walked to her patrol car.

Travis took hold of his cell phone and text Hannah, informing her that her mom had pulled him over and she knew he was just at her house. He was reading her reply when Officer Kelly returned.

The officer handed him his driver's license. "I see that you're twenty-one years of age; old enough to be drinking and going into the bars?"

"Yea.. so?"

She carried a scowl as she spoke to him. "My daughter is only sixteen. You're too old for her so I highly suggest you stay away."

Travis felt threatened and bitter towards this arrogant woman. He just wanted to drive away and never see her again.

"I'm going to let you off with a warning - about the speeding. You're free to go."

As Travis headed for home, his anger increased. Why had Hannah lied to him? Soon after entering the freeway, he exited onto Sherman Avenue and cruised Coeur d' Alene Lake Drive until the road ended with a parking area. He took hold of his cell phone and stepped out of his truck. He pressed the contact key, then Hannah's number and while he waited for the connection, he walked to the lake.

Hannah answered her phone.

Travis was fuming from his nostrils. "Is it true you're only sixteen?" he asked abruptly.

She was caught off guard by his question and because they had just been intimate with each other minutes before. "Why are you talking to me in that tone of voice like you're interrogating me?" She quickly threw back at him.

"Tone of voice? You're the one who lied to me. I have every right to be pissed!"

"Would you have gone out with me if I told you I was sixteen?"

"All I know right now is that you deceived me and I'm not happy about it." He paused. "When will you be eighteen?"

"I'm almost seventeen, so in about thirteen months."

# The New Guy

Dominique stood in front of the kitchen sink washing the leftover dishes that wouldn't fit into the dishwasher. She inhaled a deep breath and exhaled it, then dried her hands on a dishtowel. She stood erect and rubbed her lower back.

"Is your back hurting again?" Ian asked his mom after hearing her moan when he stepped into the room.

"Yea."

"That's cuz you're getting fatter in the gut."

She sent him a glare. "You don't have to be a brat about it!"

"I was just saying the truth."

"Don't you think I know."

Ian walked to the refrigerator, opened the door, and grabbed hold of the gallon of milk. He uncapped the spout and lifted the jug to his mouth.

"Get a glass!" Dominique roared.

He continued his purpose and took a gulp from the plastic container.

"You don't listen, do you?"

"Why should I?" The young teenager set the milk back into the refrigerator. "Besides, what are you going to do about it?" He returned the glare as he stepped away.

Her insides were boiling. She had had enough of his foul mouth and disobedience from the past couple of months so she reacted by grabbing a fork from the dish drainer and throwing it across the kitchen toward him. She saw that the utensil had stuck into his bottom lip.

Ian looked at her as he pulled the fork out and a drip of blood rolled down to his chin.

A rush of guilt ran through her heart. "Oh Ian." She advanced to him after grabbing a paper towel. "I didn't expect that to happen."

He handed the fork to her, then headed for the door with the paper towel. "It's okay Mom. It's just called child abuse."

"I'm sorry."

He left the kitchen.

A while later, Dominique went to check on Ian in his bedroom and found him to be lying on his bed face down. She knocked lightly on the door frame. "Can I come in?"

He spoke a muffled yes from his pillow.

She stepped to his bedside and sat at the edge of his bed. "Are you mad at me?"

"No."

She sensed her boy had been doing some crying. "I can't believe I threw that fork at you," she admitted.

"I can't believe it either." He moved his face from the imprint in his pillow and spoke in a serious tone. "You hurt my pride."

She breathed in. "I know and I'm sorry, but you were talking pretty crappy to me."

"Yea, I know." He paused. "I prayed about it though and I should of listened to you."

"Why'd you say that to me anyways?"

"I don't know. Bratty things just come over me sometimes."

She eyed the tiny scab just under his lip from where she sat. "I'm glad it didn't stick in your eye."

"Me too. I could have gone blind."

Dominique rubbed on his arm. "I prayed about it too." There was silence. "Do you want to go shopping with me? I'll buy you something special."

He thought for a moment then rolled over to his back. "Okay, I'll go, but can you bring me a glass of milk first?"

Morning came. William rounded up his team with a phone call or text. An hour later, the agents met at the Underdog's office to discuss their next bounty over a cup of coffee.

When the agents entered the office, William was sitting at his desk talking to an unknown man. Travis and Nathan sat on the couch while Nick seated himself in the chair near the marker board.

William stood. "Gentlemen, I'd like you to meet Saul. He'll be assisting our team today." He then introduced the team to Saul.

The agents observed Saul's stout frame and pop belly.

"Welcome to our team Saul," Nathan greeted.

William continued to speak as he stepped around his desk. "He's come to Idaho from San Bernardino, California. He has fifteen years experience as a bounty hunter and if he likes it here," he glanced at Saul, "he says he'll stay on permanently."

"Plus I'm too well known down there. I need a new start elsewhere," Saul added to their curiosity.

William turned to his desk and took hold of a folder. "Let's begin. Detective Parma from Orange County, California called me last night."

"I know that guy." the new agent cracked. "See what I mean?" He glanced at everyone.

William passed the mugshot of their fugitive out to his team. "This guy Laroy is bad news. He and his wife kidnapped and tortured a sixteen year old boy. Laroy somehow made bail, then took off leaving his wife to face it alone."

"What a nice guy," Travis remarked.

"His rap sheet," William explained, "says he's charged with ten counts related to the alleged abuse."

"And they let him bond out?" one agent asked.

"Yes and it's a large bond too. It says here," He shuffled to another sheet of paper, "that Laroy and his wife had at times, the teenager shackled in their home and they would beat him with sticks or a belt. The report also stated they used him as a human ashtray."

"I wanna get this scumbag already!" Saul expressed anger for their bounty.

"Me too." Travis cast his attention to William. "Let me guess. This guy fled to our part of the country and now we get to go grab him?"

"You are very smart today Travis," his boss jested with a small grin. "He has a step-brother living up Kelly Gulch and it's a strong possibility he's there." William directed Nick to advance to the marker board and draw what he had explained. "We're going to have to be clever on this one. We shouldn't call the brother and arouse any suspicion so I want to play it by ear and just go scout out the brother's place with being obvious."

Nick drew a curvy line on the marker board that resembled Kelly Gulch Road. "The houses up this gulch are spread out. I know this cuz I've been up there a many times." He marked the locations of the houses with an x, then turned to the team. "You guys will like this one. I hear we're going four-wheelin'!"

"Yay!" one voiced.

"One last thing boys," William asserted, "I looked up the brother's name with DMV and he drives a red Ford."

The crew grabbed their paperwork and gear before heading outside to the garage where the motorcycles and all-terrain vehicles were loaded onto two different trailers and awaiting their use.

Twenty minutes later at the base of Kelly Gulch, the bounty hunters parked. They exited their suv's and off-loaded the bikes. The agents outfitted themselves in their bullet proof vests, then sat on their rides. William and Travis carried pistols about their waists while Nathan and Saul took other implements for this hunt.

Nick sat as lookout in the Ford Explorer while the rest of the team sped up the gulch under the cloudy September sky. They had their route mapped out, ready to be put into action. Nathan rode side by side with William whereas Travis paired up with the new guy.

Nearly a mile into the quest, the road narrowed and turned into gravel. They observed many trails and private drives leading away from the road. William led the pack, scanning the addresses from the mailboxes at the entrance of each inlet as the rode by. "We're getting close," he shouted to Nathan.

When they came upon the next bend on the narrow road, William instructed the group to stop. He suggested Travis and Saul ride up one certain trail to scope things out while he and Nathan would take the following dirt path or private drive. "Don't get too close to the house. We don't want to scare him off," he warned his team, then transmitted their progress to Nick. "How's it going at your end? Over."

"Just sitting here, over."

He and Nathan sped further up the gulch.

Travis and Saul used caution as they maneuvered their motorcycles down into a ditch and up the dirt hillside between the tall pine trees and smaller cottonwoods. They followed the trail over dirt mounds and around large boulders until coming to a dip with several loose rocks. As he crossed, Saul's front tire hit one of the larger rocks which caused the forks to spin and he lost control, flipping over the handle bars.

Travis who was behind him, shut down and jumped off his four-wheeler. "You okay dude?" he asked as he approached the agent.

"What the hell?" He sat up in a daze and inspected himself.

"You look fine. You're not bleeding anywhere."

Saul agreed that he was fine, then stood to his feet and eyed his dirt bike. He stepped to the machine and lifted it to an upright position. He hopped onto the seat, kick started the engine, and resumed riding up the dirt path.

At the bottom of Kelly Gulch, Nick tapped his thumbs on the steering wheel of the suv as he watched for traffic to go by, especially for a red truck. He lit a cigarette and continued to wait.

William and Nathan roared up the hillside and along a ridge. At the crest, when they came to a spot within the shrubbery, they stopped and used the binoculars to spy the house thought to be Laroy's hideout.

"I don't see his truck anywhere," William spoke.

"They're probably just not home," Nathan suggested as they continued to scope the property.

They soon moved the field glasses away from their eyes and after hearing Travis and Saul cut their engines, William radioed to him of his plan. "We're leaving the bikes and headin' on foot up to the house. I want you two to do the same from your end."

The four bounty hunters scampered with caution around the scattered trees and piles of junk, over a number of small logs until coming to the outskirt of the retreat.

"We're at the house," Travis spoke quietly into the mike from the east end of the house.

"Ten-four," William replied, "We're at our end, over."

Travis and Saul peeked in through the living room and kitchen windows while William and Nathan spied the bedroom windows. "It looks to be void of any persons." Both men then stepped to the rear door and tested the knob. It was locked.

Back at the truck, Nick butted his cigarette in the ashtray, then raised a brow when he observed a red truck with two men inside cruise by, heading up Kelly Gulch Road. He sent word to the team and exited his vehicle to unhook the trailer from the explorer.

When the team heard Nick's broadcast, they backtracked to their nearest hiding spots, each pair in a different location. William and Nathan stood behind two trees at the rear of the house, whereas the other two hid alongside a camper trailer. While the four agents awaited for Laroy to arrive, Travis and Saul noticed their dirt bikes were still in sight. "Oh crap!" one exclaimed, then they heard the roar of a truck's engine coming up the private drive. Neither man had time to run and wheel them out of view.

The step-brother parked his red truck and cut the engine. Both men exited with empty hands and started walking toward the house.

Travis and Saul poked their heads out from the edge of the camper. Wanting to execute a surprise capture, they crept to the side of the house. Upon arriving, Travis tripped over a small log and bumped into the exterior wall.

Laroy stopped in his tracks when he heard the thump. He looked in that direction and noted the all-terrian vehicles.

William who was peeking at the men from his corner, advanced out from the west end of the house with his pistol aimed at the fugitive. "Freeze Laroy!" he gave command.

Laroy glanced back, then took off running, leaving his step-brother behind. He darted towards the truck, but when he saw the other two agents heading his way, he sprinted across the field and hopped onto one of the all-terrain vehicles.

Nathan who was now standing close to William, dashed away to join in the chase.

Laroy's brother stuck his foot out when Nathan passed by. Nathan went down.

Nathan jumped to his feet. "What the hell was that?" he roared as he gave the guy a push to the chest.

William stepped in between them. "You keep your cool," he told the brother.

Nathan kept a glare on the aggressor as he took two steps back, then he turned and rushed to aide in the pursuit.

William handcuffed the brother and forced him to sit on the ground with his legs crossed, then he turned to watch his team go into action.

Saul hustled to gain possession of his dirt bike while Travis and Nathan hurried across the acreage to take hold of the two other off-road vehicles.

Laroy accelerated. He sped through the backwoods, dodging trees and bushes.

Saul went after him.

Travis and Nathan rode with intense zeal for the cause of trying to corner and block in the runaway. After three attempts, it seemed as though they were just going in circles. Travis suspended his chase to jump off the ATV and grab a long stick and some egg sized stones. He climbed back onto his vehicle and piled as many stones as he could on the seat in between his legs. He sped up to join forces again with Nathan and Saul.

Laroy followed the dirt trail further into the backwoods, however, Saul was able to hinder his progress when he came to a bend in the trail by accelerating over a small mound, thrusting the bike into the air and landing on the trail seconds before Laroy drew near. Laroy had to swerve, turning his ATV sharply, causing it to nearly tip over.

Travis maneuvered in close to Laroy and started throwing stones at him, hitting him on the back and on his arms. "Shut it down!" he yelled.

The fugitive glanced back. "Kiss my ass!" He continued to ride with great force. He led the chase across a field, along the tree line and when he went around a pile of chopped wood, Saul raced about to the opposite end to try and block him. Laroy strived to avoid hitting the front tire of Saul's dirt bike, instead he turned aside and his front end nicked a tree, knocking him to the ground.

Travis and Nathan braked suddenly, skidding sideways to avoid a crash.

Laroy jumped to his feet and scampered off into the trees, however, Saul was on his tail.

Travis and Nathan abandoned their vehicles and gave chase on foot, each zigzagging around different trees and bushes to form a perimeter.

The fugitive was becoming weary in his running. His heart rate and breathing increased while his leaps and bounds decreased. Saul who was more fit, caught up and tackled him to the ground.

Laroy fought back. He grabbed a handful of dirt and cast it toward Saul's face, blinding him. He was preparing to take off again as he stood when the other two agents came running and leaped from atop of a log, thrusting themselves onto him. The lawbreaker went down hard.

# A Great Find

N ick and Nathan were in the garage behind the Underdog's office repairing and cleaning the all-terrain vehicles. Nick replaced one headlight while Nathan checked the oil levels and added gas to the fuel tanks.

Nick dropped his screwdriver twice, anxious to get the repairs done so he could head out to the lake. He thought about the fishing boat he had attached to the hitch of his truck.

Travis ignored the vibrating of his cell phone, finally shutting it off. He put it away as he sat on a stool next to a buddy, then he ordered a beer.

Hannah placed her wireless piece into the center console, belted herself in, and turned the key which started the engine to her car. She accelerated and traveled the next forty-five minutes east to the small town of Kellogg. She exited the freeway onto the Bunker Avenue ramp and drove to Travis' apartment complex. She didn't see his truck in its parking spot, yet she still stepped out of her car to test his absence with a knock at his door.

She returned to her vehicle and tried to call him once more. After leaving a brief apology for her lie on his voice mail, she drove out of the parking area with teary eyes. She wondered if he was avoiding her and would disappear out of her life?

Dominique exited the freeway near Coeur d' Alene and drove a few miles on a secondary road until coming to a paved lane that led to her beach house rental.

Nick followed behind in his own truck as he towed a boat that he rented from a friend.

After arriving at the property, Dominique and Ian climbed out of the Explorer, Ian with his remote control truck and Dominique with her guiding skills. She used them to direct Nick as he backed his trailer down to the boat ramp.

Nick let the boat rest atop of the water before he stepped out of his truck to unhook it from the trailer. He asked his mother to pull his truck and trailer up to dry land and park them while he aroused the boat's motor and propelled the craft to the dock.

Dominique stood in the driveway and watched him tie up his water toy while she text Nathan to get his eta. She looked over at Ian who had his battery operated toy at the water's edge. "Don't get that thing wet, it'll quit working!"

Almost an hour after she left Kellogg, Hannah arrived back in Hayden at her home. When she entered into the house through the anterior door, her mother was immediately in her face.

"Where were you?" Kelly exploded, "You were suppose to be her to watch your brother and start dinner!"

"He's twelve years old. He's old enough to stay here by himself for a few minutes."

"Few? I've been home for thirty minutes and besides that's not the point. When I tell you to do something, You do it!" She glared at her daughter. "You were with that Travis, weren't you?"

"No."

"Don't lie to me!"

"I'm not lying." She stepped into the kitchen.

Kelly followed her. "Where were you then?"

"Do you have to know everything? I'm almost an adult," she shot back.

"Don't get mouthy with me!"

"I went for a drive, that's all," she spoke in a softer tone. Hannah took a pound of hamburger out of the refrigerator, a pan from a lower cupboard, then stepped to the stove.

Kelly took in a deep breath and exhaled it. "I found something quite interesting today." She kept her eyes on Hannah as she stood in close.

"What did you find?" She played along in an impassive manner as she ripped open the package of hamburger.

Kelly pulled open the junk drawer and took hold of a baggie. She laid it on the counter for her daughter to see. "I suppose you're going to tell me this isn't yours?"

Hannah glanced at the content in the small bag, then cast her sights on her mother. "That's my business! I put that in the outside garbage can for my own privacy!" she snapped. "Are you going through my garbage bags now?"

Kelly quickly lifted a hand and slapped her daughter across the face. "How dare you talk to me that way!"

Her eyes became teary once again as she looked away. "Why did you tell Travis to stay away from me? I love him."

"You're too young."

"How old were you when." She had to stop and swallow the lump in her throat. "When you first fell in love?"

"Nineteen."

She knew her mom was full of crap because her mom once told her years ago about a boyfriend in high school, but before she could speak of it, Kelly changed the subject.

"The applicator is blue. Are you pregnant?" She waited to hear the answer from Hannah's lips.

She was slow to answer her yes while she crumbled a handful of the raw meat into the pan.

"Unacceptable," Kelly roared, "A baby now would ruin your life."

"How? How would love ruin my life?"

"School." she replied with sarcasm. "Taking care of a baby and a man could take your dreams away. School needs your full attention right now!"

"I'd still be able to do my schooling or anything else that came my way. I'd have Travis to help me. He has a good job..."

"No!" Kelly spoke firmly. "You're not going to have a baby. You go have an abortion. You said Travis has a good job as a bounty hunter, he can pay for it."

"No way!" Hannah thundered, "You can't make me."

"Oh yes I can. You're still a minor and he's an adult. I'll press statutory rape charges against him!"

Hannah held her mouth open in disbelief.

"That will look real good on his record," she expressed with contempt, "A sex offender bounty hunter!"

"How could you do this to me?"

"It's easy Hannah. I want what's best for you." She tossed the baggie with the blue applicator into the garbage and left the kitchen.

Fitted with a hangover, Travis still managed to make his way to the beach house to join his family for a day or two of fun. When he arrived, Nick and Nathan were drifting about the pier in the boat. He exited his truck and walked toward the wooden dock where he waited for his brothers.

Nathan climbed out of the boat and tied the rope around a pillar. He looked over at Travis. "Hey bro.. you made it."

"Barely. I drank too much last night." He paused. "You guys catch anything?"

"No. We only went for a little joyride. We're going back out in a while."

Nick stepped down from his toy onto the dock, lit a cigarette, then the three of them headed toward the house where they plopped themselves onto the patio furniture.

"So where's your girlfriend? I thought you would bring her." Nathan asked his brother.

"I'm avoiding her," he confessed.

Nick and Nathan looked at each other with tacit expressions, then at Travis, wanting his explanation.

He rubbed his forehead. "She lied to me. She's only sixteen, almost seventeen."

"Dang Travis. That's jail bait."

"That's not all. She's pregnant."

Nick chuckled. "You're in deep."

"And the worst part of it." He continued to tell them of Hannah's mother, the ill-natured cop, and the warning she gave for him to stay away from her daughter.

"Wow. Does she know Hannah's pregnant?"

"I don't think so. She just knows I'm twenty-one."

"What are you going to do?"

Travis shrugged his shoulders. "Avoid her mom."

Another minute and Dominique stepped out onto the porch to see her sons. "Everyone ready for an early lunch? I'm gonna throw some burgers on the barbecue."

"Sounds good," two replied.

"Then after an hour or so we can go out on the boat with the inner tubes, huh?"

"Yea," Nick answered.

She turned to Travis and asked him if he brought his swimming trunks.

"I did," he spoke in a sickly manner.

Travis ended up vomiting over the side of the boat and had to be brought back to shore. He walked slowly and unsteadily to the beach house then once inside, he went up the staircase and entered a spare bedroom where he laid down to nap, ending his suffering.

The boat was parked and tied. The heat of the day was upon them. Dominique and Ian swam in the luxurious swimming pool out back, then she sunbathed while the other two watched tv.

Ian headed into the house to change out his wet shorts. He went to check on his remote control truck battery and became upset with Nathan for taking his toy and using up all its power. Ian again, inserted the battery pack into the charger and plugged it into the electrical outlet, then went to the back porch to tell his mom he was going for a walk along the shoreline.

"Don't be gone too long," she advised him, "Nick's heading out on the boat after a while if you want to fish."

Ian stomped through the living room on purpose past Nathan, pushed open the screen door with a swoosh and raced out.

Bored, Nathan jumped up from the couch and followed his younger brother. "Where ya going?" he called out from the front porch.

"Don't talk to me," Ian snapped back as he kept walking. He saw from the corner of his eye, Nathan stepping slowly his way so he turned to look at him. "And don't follow me either!"

Nathan ignored his request. "It's a free country. I can walk wherever I want to." He remained at a distance as he held a cigarette in his mouth.

Ian could hear the ripples of water slapping its swell onto the rocky beach, especially after a boat sped by. He bent over to grab a shiny rock that caught his eye and put it in his pocket. He turned his head to see that his brother was still following him. Ian continued his jaunt over a small dirt trail that zigzagged through a section of beach that was consisted of pine trees and bushes. He sprang from rock to rock trying to avoid the wet ground, then the path veered away from the beach, returning to dry sand. He darted behind a tree, wanting to hide from Nathan. He waited while his breathing calmed, then he poked his head out, but didn't see him.

Nathan saw Ian hiding and crept a different way. He soon leaped around the tree into Ian's view. "Boo!" he spoofed.

"Aah.." Ian jumped.

Nathan laughed.

"You jerk!" he shot back.

"I'm sorry," he coaxed as he watched him walk off, "but that's what brother's do." He followed and soon they were talking and skipping rocks from the sandy shore into the lake. Ian threw his last flat stone, then advanced to an expanse of large boulders and climbed three of them until he rested on the smoothest one. He spied the gaps in between the boulders, searching the loose ground for more shiny rocks. A glimmer from a piece of glass captured his attention so he laid on his stomach and stretched his arm down the gap to try and grab hold of it.

Nathan watched him from another boulder. "What are you doing?"

Ian kept silent, except for the grunts he made while he struggled, moving his body as far to the rock's edge as he could go. With his fingers, he brushed the sand away from the glass and studied it. "Hmm.. A perfume bottle?" he mumbled, then wrapped his fingers around the tubular end of the device and picked it up. He scooted his torso back onto the boulder and sat up, then held his bounty in the air in front of him and examined it with an odd eye.

"It looks like a coke bottle," Nathan remarked.

The young teenager observed the blue striped bottle that had a cork in it, then eagerly expressed a thought. "What if someone wrote a sos letter and put it in here?"

"Is there a piece of paper in it?"

Ian held the glassware in the sunlight. "I can't tell. It's not a see through bottle."

"Pull the cork."

Ian placed the glass object in between his legs and extracted the cork. "Oh crap!" he roared as he released the bottle from his grip and scooted backwards, letting the bottle roll until it stopped in a depression atop of the boulder.

"No way!" Nathan blurted out when he saw the green smoke arising from the spout. His eyes widened as he watched the haze form into a female figure.

"It's.. a genie," Ian stammered, "I can't believe it!" He stood to his feet and concentrated on the spirit as it floated in the air above the bottle. The genie was staring back at him. He observed her pointy elf shoes, her sparkling green outfit that looked as though it was made of satin, then he noted her long brown hair that held a hint of white specks which twinkled like the night stars. Her countenance seemed friendly so he asked her if she was able to talk.

"My name is Felica." Her voice had a sweet angelic tone as it echoed back to him.

"Hi Felica." Even though his mind was composing a million questions, the boy didn't quite know what to ask first. Are you a real genie came out of his mouth.

"I am a real one," she replied, "You see me, right?" She moved her vision about as she eyed her new surroundings. "And what do people call you?"

"I'm Ian," He motioned with a pointed finger at himself." "And this is my brother Nathan." He then pointed his finger at his sibling.

"Thank you for releasing me Ian. I've been in that bottle way too long." Felica drifted higher and began to vigorously soar about the air. "Whew hew!" She tumbled and twisted as though she was an acrobat.

"I think she's happy to be free," Nathan spoke while they both gazed upward and watched her.

"And she seems to be a good genie and not an evil one, huh?"

"Yea."

Ian waited for the genie to stop flying. "Do I get three wishes?" he asked her.

"You are the one who freed me, so yes."

"Sweet!" Before he could ask anymore questions, he heard the faint yell of his mother calling for him. He glanced at Nathan then returned his focus in on the bewitching genie. "We have to go. Can you come home with me?"

"Is this a wish?"

"Does it have to be?" Ian challenged her.

"No. However, I'm not wanting to get back into that bottle."

Ian paused to think. "Can you make yourself invisible and follow us?"

"Is this a wish?"

He didn't want to be careless and waste a wish on something simple. "Does it have to be?" he again challenged.

She was anxious to fulfill the three wishes, but since he didn't actually say he wished it, she couldn't grant it. She sighed. "Okay, I'll get back in the bottle if you give me the cork and promise not to block the spout."

"Deal." Ian agreed.

After Felica returned to vapor form and descended into her bottle, Ian grabbed the device and with Nathan by his side, he carried his great find with him back to the beach house.

# Her Mother's Threat

Dominique and her four sons returned to their separate homes in Kellogg after a weekend of fun. Nick towed his rented boat to his friend's house and Travis who was feeling like himself again, drove to his apartment.

Following the arrival at her one acreage estate, Dominique carried her backpack into her house while Ian held his remote control truck in one hand and his striped glassware in the other. Nathan hauled in the cooler as well as his duffel bag.

"That sure is a pretty bottle you found," Dominique commented to Ian after they entered into the house.

"Yea, maybe I'll start a bottle collection." He headed toward the staircase. "I'll be in my room for a while," he told his mom, then rushed up the steps.

Nathan who didn't want to miss out on anything, took the cooler into the kitchen, then quickly joined Ian in his bedroom.

Ian locked his door, then set the genie's bottle on the carpet in the middle of his bedroom floor and rubbed the outer surface of the vessel. He stepped backwards and watched the genie arise out in smoke form, then turn human just as she did out at the lake.

Felica hovered around the room, eyeing her surroundings, including Nathan and her releasee. She pointed at the television. "What is that flat box?"

Ian answered her. "It's a tv. Do you want to see how it works?" As he kept a curious eye on her, he reached for the remote and pressed the on button.

"Ohh.." she moaned in amazement as she put her face to the screen. "There's people in there. How did they get in?" She turned to Ian for an answer.

He held a puzzled look. "You've never seen a tv before?"

"No."

He grew concerned. "How long have you been in that bottle?" He sat down on the edge of his bed and glanced at Nathan to see the interest on his face then looked again at Felica.

"A long time."

Nathan seated himself on his brother's chair and listened as he marveled over Felica's appearance.

"Where did you come from?" Ian asked her.

"It's a long story," she replied as she continued to float about inspecting Ian's trinkets.

Nathan spoke up. "We'll listen to your story if you want to tell us."

She gave him a timid smile. "I was born on a ship."

"Born?" Ian interrupted, "You weren't made?"

"I was born. That's what my ma told me."

"Where is your mother?"

"I don't know. My family and I were living with a woman named Miss Maggie on a plantation in West Virginia. She was my father's rescuer. She had wished for a black stallion and two weeks later she was thrown from it and died. Soon after that while we were sleeping one night, her brother put a cork in our bottles and separated us."

"That bastard!" Nathan replied.

"Bastard?" she questioned his foul word. "No. He didn't even know about us. I think he was just packing her things up." She paused. "I remember being in a covered wagon then on a boat.

There was ruckus on the boat, things were tossed overboard, including me. My bottle floated atop of the water, then the tides slowly carried me to the shore where I've been trapped ever since."

"So you can see out of your bottle?" Ian asked her.

"Yes it is glass."

"I couldn't see in."

Nathan cast his vision back onto the genie. "What about your parents' bottle?"

"I don't know where they're at."

"How sad," he remarked.

Ian thought more about her story, of the archaic words she had used and the lack of knowledge she had of modern technologies. "How old are you?"

"I was born in 1859."

Both fellows raised their brows. "Holy cow!" Ian exclaimed, "You're like a hundred and fifty years old."

"You don't look it," Nathan commented aloud.

"We don't age as fast as humans. In my genetics, I'm only nineteen."

"Interesting. I'm nineteen too."

Felica smiled at him, then turned her attention back to the television. "I could of used one of these in my bottle."

"What DID you do in your bottle if you don't mind me asking?" Nathan asked her.

"I read a lot, slept, played with my dolls, and.. I also exercised – practiced my ballet."

"It kind of sounds like being in jail, except for the dolls and ballet part."

She continued to watch the screen while the guys watched her.

"How long do I have to make my three wishes?"

"There's no time limit," she answered Ian.

Its almost like deja' vu Hannah thought as she asked Travis where he's been. She was concerned, yet she presented herself to be demanding as they greeted each other on their cell phones.

"I was on a bounty," he defended himself, "then I went up to my mom's beach house for a couple of days. So what?" He sat on his couch with his television on mute.

"Why didn't you at least call me?"

"I tried.. I couldn't get any bars out at the lake and then my phone died. I didn't have my charger with me." Travis lowered his head in shame. He didn't want to admit he was avoiding her.

She sensed some deceit. "Are you mad at me?"

"No Baby. I guess I've just been doing some thinking about things."

She paused. "I need to talk to you – in person."

He couldn't resist her charm. The charm he knew she carried deep within her heart. "I'll come to Hayden. Where do you want to meet?"

"You can come to my house. My mom's at work."

"Oh no.. She'll probably come home and I don't want to hide in the closet again."

Hannah chuckled. "She won't be coming home unannounced. She's dispatching this evening."

They said their quick I love you's and ended their call, then Travis changed his clothes, styled his hair, and thought about slapping cologne on his face, but decided not to. He left in his truck and headed over the mountain pass.

Hannah sent her brother down the street to his friend's house, then fashioned herself for Travis' eyes.

An hour and a half had past by when Travis arrived at her house. He parked his truck down the street and walked the sidewalk to the anterior door, then knocked.

She opened the movable structure and greeted him. She had her hair in an updo and she wore a silvery mist color of eye shadow that brought out the gray in her blue eyes.

"You look beautiful," he choked up, then handed her a flat box that was wrapped and fit with a small bow.

"Oh Baby!" she cooed. "This is the best thing that's happened to me all week." She felt her eyes becoming glazed with a tear. She fought it off as she gave him a kiss. After inviting him to come into the house, she shut and locked the door, then led him to the living room where she was going to open her gift. They sat on the couch that was located in front of the large window so she could keep watch at the traffic.

Travis nudged her to open the box.

She lifted the lid. "Ohh.. They're pretty." She took hold of the paper butterfly and raised it into view. It had a clear string attached to it followed by another decorated butterfly and more string, then a third butterfly; all five butterflies were glittery and colored differently. "I love them."

"You're welcome," he spoke as he leaned into her and kissed her neck.

She giggled. It had felt good to smile, yet inside, she dreaded having to break the news of her mother's threat to him.

"You want to go horse around?"

"What?" She hadn't heard that phrase before.

"Hhhuuhhhuu.." he neighed like a horse close to her ear.

"You're silly." She was laughing. "I don't really want to right now, Babe. We need to talk."

"Okay. Let's go outside so I can smoke."

They went outside to the back porch where he first lit his cigarette. He positioned his back against the wooden rail, lifted and set the sole of his foot onto a post. She stood beside him, facing the yard with her arms resting on the flat railing. She was silent as she sought in her mind for the right words. She felt as though she wanted to vomit and her voice shook as she began to speak. "I have bad news. Really bad news." She didn't even want to look him in the eye.

"You're not breaking up with me, are you Baby?"

"No."

He took a drag from his cigarette as he waited for her to speak. She inhaled big. "My mom found out that I'm pregnant."

He looked at her with much concern. He knew that her mother was an aggressive and unpredictable woman, however, he still asked, "How is that really bad news?"

Her eyes became clouded with tears. "She told me I had to get an abortion."

Travis' eyes widened. "What?" He couldn't believe what she had just said. "Did I hear you right?"

She nodded.

"She has no right. That's our baby!"

"I'm only sixteen – remember?"

He raised his brow and slowly moved his head to the right, to the left, then back to the right. "So?"

"She threatened to press charges of statutory rape against you if I didn't get one."

"That witch!" He hardened his jaw in displeasure. "How did she find out you were pregnant?"

Hannah burst out crying. "I'm sorry. She went snooping in my garbage can." She dropped to her knees and covered her face with her hands.

Travis flipped his cigarette out onto the lawn and knelt beside her. "You don't have to cry Baby." He wrapped his arms around her to try and comfort her. "We'll get through this."

"She slapped me Travis. I hate her." She continued to sob.

Travis understood the hatred she was feeling, however, he hadn't known that feeling toward a parent. "I'm sorry she did that to you."

Hannah used her shirt to wipe her tears.

Travis stood to his feet and while he stepped about the porch, he became angrier with every new and different thought. At that moment, a surge of violence traveled through his body so he lifted his leg and used his heel to kick one of the wooden posts. "How dare she slap you and force you to get an abortion."

"Oh crap!" Hannah burst out when the post broke away from the railing.

"That was your mom's face!"

Hannah stood to her feet and stepped to the post. She tried to push it back into place while Travis stepped back and lit another cigarette. "I'll have to use a hammer on it," she pointed out.

There was a moment of silence, then Travis spoke, "I don't want to go to jail."

She cast her vision onto him and saw that he wore a serious look, then she turned her eyes away from him. "It'll cost five hundred dollars."

Dominique gathered the boxes that contained her three published novel titles and set them with her posters and display board close to the door in her office. She glanced at the clock, then walked out to the living room and stood near the bay window.

Ian dashed in through the anterior door of the house after being dropped-off out front by the school bus. "Hi Mom! Is Nathan here?" he asked as he hurried for his bedroom.

"No. He was called to work."

"Darn it." He turned and ran up the staircase.

"Hey?" She raised her voice, "Are you still going with me Saturday to my book signing?"

He stopped on the top step. "Ohh.. do I have to?"

She had an odd look upon her face. "I thought you wanted to go with me?"

"I want to hang out with Nathan. It's our brother day," he fabricated.

"Mm-hm. Sounds suspicious to me," she commented as she watched him disappear into the hallway and beyond.

Ian closed the door and scanned his room for his genie. He didn't see her floating about so he stepped to her bottle and rubbed it. She didn't flow upward.

"I'm over here."

"Huh?" He turned his eyes toward the voice and saw Felica changed from an invisible state to her normal self. She was sitting on his bed. "You can be invisible! How do you do that?"

"I don't really know. It's just part of being a genie."

He advanced to his game chair and when he sat, he sat facing her. "I know what my first wish will be, but I can't ask for it until Saturday."

# Stairs to Nowhere

Three of the team members gathered around the conference table to discuss their next bounty. While William stood near, he handed each agent a photo of the fugitive.

"I have a report here," Saul began, "of a young man who started out being kicked out of school, he's spent time in juvenile detention, then jail and he's been a troublemaker ever since." He looked up at William.

William faced the marker board and began to write down some descriptions. "His name is Aaden. He's five feet, seven inches and weighs a hundred and seventy pounds." He glanced down at the file. "His hair is different from the photo because he's shaved it off." As he continued to talk, he stepped about. "Aaden has three warrants and according to his father, Aaden's probation officer is too busy. The father wants his son found and taken to jail so he can clean up and get help. He's revoking the bond to do so." William paused. "I think Aaden won't be too hard for you guys to catch. It's only Wallace so I'm just sending you three on this one." He glanced at Travis and Nathan as he handed the file to Saul.

Saul flipped through the folder and took hold of Aaden's rap sheet. He read it aloud in his deep voice. "Multiple assault charges and malicious crimes, mostly misdemeanors. And I see that his recent charges are drunk and disorderly, assault on an officer - again," he emphasized, "and resisting arrest."

"He could fight us upon capture," Nathan cautioned.

Saul grinned, showing the gap from his missing teeth. "I love a good fight," he bragged, "I'll just show that punk my 50 caliber and he'll be begging us to take him in."

The Underdog's didn't dress up in their regular uniformed shirt for this hunt. Instead, they only outfitted themselves with bullet proof vests underneath t-shirts and handcuffs on the back of their belts.

"Text me when you got him," William called out.

The bounty hunters concealed their badges in their pockets as they withdrew to the outdoors. They hopped in the company suv, then headed to Wallace.

Within the small historic town, Saul parked alongside a curb across the street from their destination. While he stayed in the vehicle to spy, Travis and Nathan took a glance at their fugitive's photo and exited. They advanced upon the pavement, then the sidewalk to the door of the secured apartment building of Aaden's last known address and tried the knob.

"It's locked," one said.

"Now what?"

Aaden searched in vain for his cell phone among his scattered clothes and disorganized items in his apartment. "Where the hell did I put it?" he rebuked himself to his pal Caleb. "My girlfriend is suppose to be calling me any minute."

"Just wait for it to ring then you'll know where it's at," Caleb spoke with confidence as he remained on the couch playing his video game.

"I turned the sound off."

"Sounds like you're fucked then!" he shot back.

Aaden groaned as he sent his friend a scowl. "Will you help me look?"

"No.. I didn't lose your phone."

He grabbed a shoe from the floor and threw it towards him. When the sneaker hit the couch, his cell phone flew out of it, landing on the cushion. "Whoa! Did you see that?"

Caleb glanced at the phone, then at Aaden. They both chuckled.

"I just sent him a text," Travis said to Nathan his co-worker and brother.

"What did you say?"

"I told him to come open the door. I'm with Fed-ex and I have a delivery for him."

"Yeah, we'll see if that works," Nathan spoke with skepticism. "But I doubt it."

Travis agreed.

The agents waited five minutes with no response, then a tenant who lived at that same address approached the main door from the inside and exited the building. Travis grabbed the door before it closed so they could enter in. They went up the staircase toward Aaden's apartment to his door. Nathan leaned in, putting his ear close for a listen before knocking.

Caleb who was now standing among friends in a neighbor's apartment, peered out the peephole from across the hall when he heard the knocking. "Oh dude," he whispered to Aaden with a turn of his head. "Someone's at your door."

Aaden took a peek at the two men. "They're probly the ones who text me."

"Do you know who they are?"

"No." He paused a moment to think. "Follow me." Aaden led the way through his neighbor's apartment to a rear window and opened it. He climbed out onto the steel structure and descended the rusty ladder.

Nathan looked at Travis. "I don't think anyone's home."

Travis again beat on the hardwood door. "Open up Aaden!" he shouted.

Further up the hall, a door creaked open and an Asian man poked his head through the gap to see who was yelling.

"Hey?" Travis hastened toward him. "I'm a bounty hunter and I'm searching for your neighbor Aaden." He withdrew the photo and showed the man.

"No, no, I not see him today." The man retreated into his apartment and closed the door.

Travis glanced at Nathan. "I have an idea," he spoke as he turned, then walked to the door opposite of Aaden's apartment with his mugshot in hand, then knocked.

The door was opened by a young man who seemed to be high and the scent of marijuana drifted out into the corridor.

The Underdogs could see into the dwelling, the many guests who were either standing or sitting. "We're looking for Aaden," one spoke loudly.

"He just went out the back window!" one in the crowd blurted out.

The other man's reply seemed real so the bounty hunters took off running down the hall toward the staircase. Travis radioed to Saul of Aaden's slick move and suggested he drive in the alleyway to try and spot him. The two agents darted down the steps and exited the building. They entered the alley just as Saul was advancing in the suv. With no sign of Aaden anywhere, the agents hastened to the next block. They rounded the corner at the border of a reddish brick building then slowed their pursuit when they came upon Bank Street. While Saul cruised the nearby streets, they sat on a wooden bench and scanned the area. "I'm going to call him. Maybe he'll answer this time."

Aaden and Caleb entered the local supermarket. They walked in two different aisles before picking out soda pops to purchase. They left the store and when they stepped behind the building, Aaden's cell phone rang. He looked at the number. "It ain't my girl calling." Out of curiosity, he lifted the flip and answered it.

"Where are you Aaden?" Travis demanded.

"Who wants to know?" he shot back.

"The Underdogs bounty team. You need to tell me where you're at so we can meet up."

"Why?"

"We need to discuss your warrants."

"What? I don't have any warrants," he played.

"Then there's no problem with you meeting up with us right now – over on Bank Street. Come show your face!"

"No. I don't want to."

"Why not?"

"I just don't want to. If you want to talk to me, you'll have to come find me first," he offered with a cocky tongue, the ended the call.

Travis looked at Nathan after he closed his cell phone. "I'm not wanting to race all over town on foot chasing this jerk."

"It's our job. We might have to."

Travis looked away and reached for the cell phone in his pocket. He dialed for Saul to drive his way.

Another half minute and Saul pulled up alongside the curb in front of the bench where Travis and Nathan were sitting.

The two agents arose and stepped to the truck. Travis leaned in through the open window and lifted Aaden's file from the seat. He skimmed through it, looking for another address that may have been missed. He found no other.

"What now?" Nathan questioned.

"Let's go show his mugshot around in front of the store."

While the two rookies hastened across the street, Saul parked the explorer in the grocer's parking lot. He exited the vehicle with a photo of the fugitive and went inside the store to ask both clerks if they'd seen him recently.

"He was in here about ten minutes ago with a buddy," one replied.

"Can you tell me what he was wearing?"

She thought a moment. "A white t-shirt and blue jeans. He was wearing his jeans low around his butt and you could see his boxers sticking out."

Saul smiled. "Did you happen to see which way he went once he left the store?"

"He headed around towards the back of the building," the clerk answered as she pointed.

Saul walked out of the store and as he approached his team, he observed them to be talking to a woman who was telling them of Aaden's girlfriend.

"She lives over on Cedar Street, a few houses down from the post office."

"What's her name?"

"Abby." The woman answered then backed off.

Saul edged in and turned his attention to Travis and Nathan. "Let's head over to this Abby's house and see if he's there."

"He would have had to run."

Saul reached into his jeans pocket and withdrew the keys. "Maybe we'll get lucky – if we hurry." They retreated to the suv, climbed in, then drove through the parking lot to the road that went around the supermarket looking for any traces of Aaden. They came out on Bank Street and followed it around the block to Cedar Street. They turned left and parked in front of the post office.

"There's only two houses he could be at," Nathan guessed as he scoped the neighborhood with the binoculars.

"Let's start knocking on doors then," Travis urged.

The agents exited the suv with the portable radios and while Saul hastened to the alleyway to stand guard, the other two agents walked the sidewalk to the first house and approached the door.

An elderly man with streaks of red within his gray hair opened the door. The agents showed him Aaden's picture as they inquired of him.

"I've seen him before over yonder." He gestured with a nod of his head toward the house next door.

The bounty hunters quickly thanked him, then turned and walked fast out of his yard. Travis radioed to Saul of their next move. "Be ready.. we're waling on the sidewalk now, over."

A vehicle slowed and stopped suddenly alongside the curb, grabbing the agents attention. Aaden's father called out to the two agents from the passenger's side window.

Travis and Nathan turned and stepped to the car.

"William said over the phone that you guys were in Wallace today looking for Aaden. I just saw him over by the Conoco. He tried ducking from me."

"He is a fast runner!" one agent spoke to the other then addressed the father. "We're on it!"

Aaden's father drove off.

Travis transmitted to Saul into the mike for him to race back to the truck; they have a lead on Aaden.

"Ten-four. I'm running now."

All three men jumped into the suv and sped off. They drove the back roads to the named business and parked in the large lot between it and a motel. On the north and south sides of them were the hillside and the old highway that runs parallel to the river.

"I'm going inside!" Travis spoke as he looked at his comrades, particularly Nathan. "I think you should go behind the building and come around the other side." The two rookies darted to their positions while William kept himself ready at the wheel. Travis left his gun in the explorer, not wanting to scare the customers.

Aaden and Caleb were resting up on the hillside within the thicket when they observed Travis and Nathan crossing the pavement and sneaking about. "That's them." Aaden stated. "Let's get going." He arose and led Caleb further up the hillside away from the gas station. "We'll hide for a while and they'll get tired of searching and leave."

"You think it's as simple as that? They're bounty hunters, right Aaden? They'll call for reinforcements," Caleb cautioned as he followed behind, taking a wide step over a downed log.

"Maybe, unless we can get far off at a distance." He continued to trek the forest away from the agents.

Travis and Nathan returned to the suv. "He's not in there," Travis told Saul then scanned the area, including the hillside as he stood within the open door of the explorer. "I bet he either caught a quick ride out of here or he's up on that hillside." He jumped into the suv and sat.

"If he is, he'll probably stay close to the highway." Saul accelerated out of the parking lot, out onto the old highway. He drove slow on the shoulder of the road scooping the hillside for their fugitive. "Well boys.." He paused for a drag from his cigarette. "Looks like you two get to go hiking." He stopped the vehicle.

Travis was the first to step out of the suv. He strapped his holster to his waist and grabbed the portable radio, then he and Nathan crossed the barren highway.

Saul drove a bit further up the road and parked within an inlet. He spied the hillside for Aaden and the team through his binoculars.

Aaden had to stop and pant for air. He turned his head back to look in the direction he just came to observed his distance.

Caleb who was following, also halted to catch his breath. "How far you really going cuz I'm not the wanted man. They don't want me." He took a swig from his water bottle.

"Just go with me a little farther," he urged, "Then we'll slow down."

The agents came upon a stone wall after crossing the four lane highway. They glanced to the left and to the right. At the end of the stone wall they noticed a passageway. They jogged to it and began their uphill trek.

"Check this out!" Nathan called out after he climbed a few feet. "A set of old steps."

Travis paused and gave heed to the fungi and old cement.

They advanced up the moss covered stairway until its end at the top flat section of the hill. They stood idle while they caught their breath. The breeze helped to cool their faces.

"Stairs to nowhere," Nathan remarked.

"There was probably a house or building here long ago," Travis pointed out.

The agents cast their eyes about the thicket. They used their mini binoculars to try and detect any movement. Travis inhaled deep. "I smell cigarette smoke." He told Nathan then sent an action report back to Saul.

"Ten-four. And I'm not seeing any movement from down here, over."

Nathan sniffed the air and detected the scent as well. "That way." He pointed eastward as he led the way. They quietly stepped into the grove and after advancing some thirty yards, each agent stood behind their own large tree. They peeked beyond the tall firs to scope the vicinity, then waited.

Soon enough, the bounty hunters caught a glimpse of their fugitive approaching at a snail's pace in between the pine trees and in through the brush. Travis drew his pistol and stood tall against his tree while Nathan prepared the handcuffs. They heard the crunching of twigs and leaves from Aaden and Caleb's footsteps as they draw near. When they were close enough, Travis stepped out from beyond his tree with his weapon aimed directly at Aaden.

Aaden froze when he saw the two agents. His eyes widened. "Are you kidding me?" he cracked.

# A Wish in Time

Saturday morning was upon Dominique and her family. Dominique giggled as she watched her two new kittens chase and play with each other upon the tiled floor. One would hike up her back to make herself appear larger to the other cat, then walk sideways. Dominique never thought she'd own any pets, but after Ian brought one home from the neighbor's house last week to show her, she fell in love with the tailless black one. The other cat that was also black was the boys' favorite. They named her Cobra.

Just when Cobra playfully attacked her sister, Nick entered into the kitchen. "I knocked," he told his mom, but could see she was fully engrossed in watching the young felines.

Dominique glanced at her son. "Oh.. hey Nick," she greeted.

"They're cute," he remarked as he sat onto a chair.

"They are, huh? I love that manx kitty the best." She paused. "So how's work going?"

"It's going good. Finished roofing that new house up on the hill yesterday."

"Nice. Hopefully you made bank on it?"

"Yea, I did good."

"Awesome," she commented, "Now it's my turn to make bank – again."

"You're off to your book signing now?"

"Here in a bit."

"Do you need help setting up?"

"No. Not this time. They have helpers at this event."

"Well can I stay here today? I'll babysit your kittens," he asked in a persuasive tone.

She thought a moment. "I guess so. You know my house rules, plus Nathan and Ian will be here all day too – I think."

Nathan and Ian were just emerging from their bedrooms when Dominique bid them good-bye. She stated to Ian that she expected him to stay out of trouble while she's away, then she closed the anterior door, walked the sidewalk to her explorer, and drove off, making her was to a nearby town.

Ian left his unfinished breakfast at the table and hurried upstairs to his bedroom. Nathan followed, leaving Nick in the kitchen with the kittens. Ian closed his bedroom door, then stepped to the blue striped bottle. While Nathan sat at the foot of his bed, he scooted the bottle closer to the edge of the shelf and called for his genie. "Felica?" he spoke softly into the spout.

Felica arose from the bottle and showed herself.

Ian stepped backwards. He and Nathan both noticed she wasn't wearing her usual sparkling blue outfit, but rather a sparkling red one.

"You're looking good!" Nathan blurted.

She sent a timid smile his way, then focused in on Ian.

"I'm ready for my first wish," he stated to her.

"I'm ready to grant it."

There was a knock at his bedroom door. Felica evolved into her state of invisibility.

Nick popped open the door. "Hey bro.." He looked at Nathan. "Come smoke a bowl with me."

"I will later," he assured, anxious to hang out with Felica and learn of his younger brother's wish.

Nick observed the stillness in the room and grew suspicious. "What's going on?"

"Nothing Dude. I just don't want to get stoned yet."

"Okay." he stretched his word of approval, then closed the door. Felica reappeared and fixed herself in a sitting position amidst the air.

Ian spoke. "My wish is to go back in time to see my dad. Both me and Nathan."

"Wow!" she expressed surprise. "Why go back? Can't you see him now?"

"No." His speech grew faint. "He died when I was just a small kid."

Felica turned to Nathan. "What about you? How old were you?"

"Seven."

She thought for a moment. "Any particular date or place you want to go?"

"I'd like to see my dad when he was about my age, around 1975."

Nathan cut in. "He grew up in Pinehurst."

"Pinehurst?" She exhibited confusion.

"Pinehurst, Idaho. Here in America." Ian explained with an amused countenance. "It's only five miles from here."

"As you wish." Felica arose from her sitting position and as she floated vertically, she gestured for Nathan to stand as well. She began to twirl that turned into a spin.

Ian's mouth hung open as he watched her start to fade. He felt himself becoming weightless, as though he had no gravity holding him down.

Nick opened the door and when he stepped into the room, he was vaporized out of the current time with his brothers.

The fellows and Felica came into existence upon the dirt ground in Pinehurst. Ian and Nathan took notice of Felica who was standing with them wearing blue jeans and a top. They also saw Nick.

"What the hell Nick?" Nathan thundered, "What are you doing here?"

Nick was speechless, at first. "I don't know," he shot back with innocence. "You tell me. I just opened Ian's bedroom door and stepped into his room, then bam! I'm here with you."

Everyone was quiet.

"This is Ian's genie," Nathan told Nick.

"Nice." he remarked, "After mom's magic mirror seven years ago, I believe it."

Ian and Nathan scanned the area and saw familiar businesses within the shopping complex. "Where's Gary's Drug store? It's not even built!" one stated with wonder.

"Everything else looks mostly the same, but newer."

"I agree," another answered as they walked towards the north end of the parking lot near the grocery store.

"Check out that old Datsun and that Dodge Charger! It's not a 69, but it's still cool," Nick boasted because he thought himself to be the car guy in the family. "And there's a Pinto and a Chevy Vega – Awesome!"

Felica was uneducated to the modern invention of the automobile. She was quiet as she listened, figuring she would study up on things later.

Nathan patted his empty pockets and realized he hadn't grabbed his cigarettes. He turned to Nick. "You got your smokes on you?"

"Oh shit! I don't," he answered as he touched his own pockets.

"I have some cash. I'll just go buy a pack." He pulled his wallet out and sifted through a few bills. He took hold of a five.

Ian observed the legal tender from where he stood. "That's a new five. The store will think it's a fake and not take it."

"Smart thinkin' there kid brother!"

Nathan returned the five to his wallet and drew out a one dollar bill. "It's the only old one I have. I hope a pack of cigarettes is under a buck?"

"It might be," Nick commented.

A couple of minutes later, Nathan returned from the grocery store and lit one of his cigarettes, then handed one to Nick. "They didn't even card me!" After he took a drag, he looked at Ian. "So.. what's your plan?"

"I don't know. Let's walk to Grandma's house and see if our dad is around."

"It's only ten in the morning. He's probably sitting on the couch in his pj's watching cartoons and eating Cocoa Pebbles."

"No it's not," Felica asserted, "I brought you to the afternoon. You feel that hot sun?" She expanded her arms.

The guys looked upward and noted the glow.

"Yes, I'm starting to sweat," one spoke.

Nick pulled his cell phone out from his pocket and pushed up the slider. "My phone is dead. It's not even showing the time or date."

"There's no towers!" Nathan exclaimed, "or satellites in 1975?"

"I don't know." Nick shrugged his shoulders.

"It's about four o'clock." Felica said, then informed them briefly of how to use the sun to tell time.

The group went east on Country Club Lane. On one side of the street there were houses and behind them was unsettled acreage dressed with sparse trees and bushes. On the other side lay a golf course. Beyond that a hill outlined the field and fairway.

When the foursome passed by the only vacant lot, Ian noticed two teenage boys in the field behind his grandmother's house. "That could be him." He pointed out to his brothers.

"Let's go over there."

"What are we gonna say to him?"

Nathan exhaled. "We definitely won't be telling him we're his sons."

"Yea." Ian chuckled., "Cuz you're older than him right now."

The young men and their genie veered from the road into the vacant lot.

"Hey guys," Felica announced, "I'll be invisible for a while."

They watched her fade away. "Can you still hear us talk?" Ian asked her.

"Yes," she whispered.

"Mmm.." Nathan murmured to himself. He loved the sound of her soft sexy voice.

As the two thrill seekers approached their young dad, Ian felt butterflies in the pit of his stomach. What if his dad, he thought, wanted to cause trouble. He had heard that he was popular in school and always tried to be tough so nobody would pick on him. Ian didn't want his first wish to be for nothing.

They observed Andrew and his friend to be carrying boards away from his home into a patch of tall bushes out in the field.

Andrew and his friend Samuel stopped and set their pieces of wood down. Andrew eyed the group seeing they were older boys. "What do you guys want?" he asked.

Nick, Nathan, and Ian stood idle. Ian's jaw was slightly dropped as he scanned his dad's face, trying to match up his features with his own or Nathan's.

"Are these your cousins?" Samuel turned to Andrew in question. "They look like you."

"No," he replied.

"We're new in town," Nick spoke. "Just walking around, checking things out."

Andrew observed Nathan's pack of cigarettes he had tucked away in his t-shirt pocket. "What's your names?"

Nathan told him their first names only.

"I'm Andrew and this is Samuel. Can I have one of your cigarettes?"

"Sure." He looked down at his pocket and grabbed his pack. He thought it was cool to give his dad one. "You need a light too?"

"No." He held the cigarette in a closed fist and followed Samuel who carried two boards toward the bushes.

"You guys building a fort?" Ian asked.

"Yea."

Nick watched the two teenage fathers walk away, then he stepped to Nathan. "That's MY Dad!" he whispered.

"I figured so," he replied as he lit a cigarette for himself.

The three brothers hung out for a half an hour helping to nail together a set of 2 by 4's before Andrew was called in to dinner.

Andrew turned to his two new older buddies and Ian. "What are you guys doing in a couple of hours?"

It was dark when Ian and his brothers met up with their dads in the midst of the golf course on the green. They were sitting around the hole; Nick and Nathan smoked on cigarettes.

"Hey gentlemen," Andrew cracked when he and Samuel approached with their flashlights and joined them in their circle. "I didn't know if you guys would really show up."

"Yea – we're here. Got nothing better to do," one replied.

There was some odd silence.

"I have a joint." Nick offered.

"Light it up!" Andrew shot back, trying to fit in.

Everyone except Ian smoked. He just eyed his dad through the darkness, awed with sorrow that he smoked at such a young age, yet he didn't dwell on it long.

"Want to have some fun?" Andrew's tone was to excite them.

"What you got in mind?" Nick questioned.

"I got keys to the golf carts."

"What? Where did you get keys?" Nick popped with interest while Nathan and Ian turned their faces toward one another and through the moonlight they observed each others agreement with a nod.

"I stole them yesterday."

"I'm in. Let's go!" one instigated the crowd.

The gang arose to t heir feet and headed toward the pro shop. Andrew and Samuel who were familiar with the doors and landscape, led the way. Andrew opened the first garage door and crept in. He turned on his flashlight and handed a key to Nick, then one to Nathan. Nathan and Ian sat onto one while their dad and Samuel shared the second cart and Nick followed in the third.

"This is like a go-kart, but only quieter," Ian boasted from the passenger's seat.

"That's because it's powered by electricity and not gas," he answered Ian as he sped through the open garage door.

Andrew led them to the far corner of the course, away from the houses and town streets, then braked.

Nathan and Ian came up alongside their dad and stopped. "This is fun! You guys do this often?" the eldest asked with a chuckle.

"No. This is our first time."

Nick steered his cart in too close to the side of his brothers' cart and caused it to bump. He laughed.

"Oh you dog! So that's how you wanna play, huh?" Nathan cast a glance at him, then turned his head forward and stomped on the pedal. "Whew-hew!" Ian held on.

Nick took off after him as did Andrew and Samuel.

Nathan steered his vehicle around in a loop with intentions of exerting a side swipe to Nick's cart. After a couple of attempts, he collided into the buggy while Andrew and Samuel smacked onto Nick's other side.

"Double whammy!" Nick roared upon impact, then maneuvered himself free.

Nathan drove forward, tapping his dad's cart as he sped off.

"Let me drive," Ian bid to his brother.

"No way!" Nathan replied, "This is too much fun."

"It's my wish, remember?"

After a moment of pause, he complied. "Okay Ian, but you can't be a chicken."

They switched places, then Ian pressed the pedal down. "I can't hardly see them. Where's the headlights on this thing?"

"There's no headlights."

Ian heard a crash and headed in that direction. With just a peek from the moonlight, he saw a cart approach him so he swerved out of the way. He circled back and set his sights on the closest victim, then made contact. "Bam!" Ian blurted when he hit. His opponent's cart tipped over.

"Far out!" Andrew shot as he rolled up to the scene and watch Nick stand to his feet from the inside of the golf cart. "You okay?"

"Yea."

The gang took to their feet and surrounded the fallen cart. They lifted and returned it to its tires.

Nick lit a cigarette and hopped back into his buggy. He drove it up the small mound. "It's steering funny," he called out.

The boys played chase and demolition derby for some two minutes before one spotted a man standing at the roadside by his car, shining a high beam light about the expanse. "Oh shit – It's a cop!"

The gang braked to take a gander.

"Time to go!" Nathan cautioned as he urged Ian to drive back towards the garage in the opposite direction of the patrolman.

"Wait!" Nick called out for their attention. "There could be another cop over there. I'm gonna head this way." He recommended to the group to do the same. He moved the bar to direct his buggy back toward the far corner of the fairway.

Ian heeded his brother's advice and turned his cart around, then accelerated toward the far corner behind him.

"That's the hillside!" Andrew grumbled, ignoring what anyone was saying. He thought he was following Ian's cart as he sped from the greatest distance toward the garage.

Ian was topped out at full speed when Andrew's cart suddenly came upon him. "Oh crap!"

Andrew swerved to avoid a head-on collision and clipped a nearby tree with the front end, forcing the cart to totter and flip.

Ian stomped on the brake, then he and Nathan ran to see if their dad and Samuel had been hurt.

"I think my elbow's scraped up."

The four bandits noticed the policeman had jumped in his squad car and drove back down the street to the Pro shop area. They watched him drive beyond the entrance out onto the green.

"Run!"

They left the golf carts and hastened to the dark mountainside.

The officer clicked on his bright lights and headed east toward the ruckus.

The lawbreakers rushed to the nearby shrubbery. Each entered at separate locations; Ian followed Nathan, Andrew tailed Samuel, and Nick went solo. They slinked up the hillside between the pine trees and brush. At one point, Nathan and Ian had to stop and catch their breath. While they were crouched under a tree, they watched the officer shine his spotlight onto the golf carts, then when he turned the beam of light up onto the hillside, they ducked.

"I can't believe this," Nathan whispered to his brother, "Here I am a bounty hunter and I'm hiding from a cop!"

"It happens," Ian replied, not quite knowing what to say.

When the policeman aimed his light in a different direction, Nathan and Ian continued uphill until they came to a dirt lane.

"Where you guys been?" Nick asked as he drew on a cigarette.

"Hiding."

"Yea," Nick chuckled, "Me too."

Andrew stepped to the gang and bummed another cigarette.

After a half an hour, the bandits observed the squad car as it turned away and migrated west. "Me and Samuel are gonna sneak back to my house now," Andrew told them. "Silence is the word – Nobody talks about this night to anyone, okay?"

"No problem," Nick stated.

"See you guys later." Andrew and Samuel turned and headed down the street.

"Bye Andrew," Ian addressed as he watched his dad disappear into the darkness. His heart sank because he knew he wouldn't see him again until years later when he, himself would die and go to heaven. "I love you dad," he spoke under his breath, yet only Nathan heard him.

The three brothers stepped slowly down the street as well. The sky rendered a bolt of lightning, then offered another. "I think it's going to rain. I can smell it." Nick inhaled deep through his nostrils. "Yap – rain."

"Felica?" Ian sought after.

"I'm here," she answered as she appeared.

"Where were you?"

"I've been here. I was lying on top of your roof during your demolition derby. I went tumbling and soaring twice through the air."

Nick and Nathan laughed. "Awesome."

A rumble of thunder roared about the sky. Ian cast his eyes beyond the golf course toward his grandmother's house and with the aid of the porch light, he happened to see his dad and Samuel cross the driveway and exit around the corner of the house. "Felica. We're ready to go home."

Nick cleaned up after the two kittens and changed their water dish before he left in his truck for home.

Ian showered and when he descended the staircase to the living room, his mom was just walking through the anterior door carrying a box. "Hi Mom. How was your book signing?"

"Amazing. I sold ten books." She closed the door. "How was your day? Nobody text me."

"Sorry I didn't, but my day was good too. I hung out with Nathan like we had planned." He followed his mom to her office. "I wanted to ask you a question about my dad."

"Okay, ask away." She set her box of leftover books onto the floor in the corner.

"Did my dad ever tell you if he stole anything big when he was a teenager?"

"Anything big?"

"Yea, like a car or any type of vehicle?" He was trying to avoid saying golf cart.

There was silence as she thought. "I don't think he ever stole a car or motorcycle."

He paused. "What about a boat or golf cart. He did live by a golf course."

"Yes he did," she recalled.

Ian grinned. "What happened?"

"All he said was that he and some buddies stole a couple of golf carts and went joyriding. They got caught a few days later when Samuel, Nick's dad, went to school and bragged about it."

# Out Back

The summer came to an end and Ian was heading back to school. He would now be in the highest grade in the Kellogg Middle School.

Dominique dropped off the well dressed eighth grader, then returned home where she engaged in twenty laps in her indoor pool before showering and going to her home office for a morning of writing.

"Hey Mom." Nathan poked his head in. "I'm off to work now."

"You're getting a late start." She cast her attention toward him. "Be safe."

He began to leave.

"Hey?" she called out.

He stepped back into the doorway.

"You'll be working with that new guy?"

"Yea, why?"

She shrugged her shoulders. "No reason really."

Nathan grew suspicious of her question. He came to realize that his single mother may be interested in Saul. "I'll tell him you said hi."

"No!" she spoke up immediately.

He grinned. "Just kidding, but soon you'll have to meet him."

Nathan arrived at the Underdog's Bounty Hunting office at the same time as Saul. They entered the building and saw William sitting at his desk. Nathan looked around for his brother.

"Travis called off today," William informed the team. "It's just us three."

"What about Nick?" Saul queried.

"I already tried him. He has to be at his roofing job today."

The three agents sat around the conference table with a file and their cell phones.

"Swade has a guy who didn't go to court. His name is Brett Willoughby. I e-mailed each of you his picture a while ago."

"I got mine," one answered.

Saul looked at his phone. "He's one ugly dude!"

"He doesn't have too bad of a rap sheet, however, he is facing some prison time," William continued.

"That's why he's running," one commented.

"I agree. We have to catch this fugitive because Swade has a large bond on him." William flipped through a few pages from the file. "Brett's got two weapon's charges against him so he could be armed. Let's gear up, we're heading to Coeur d' Alene."

Travis jumped in his truck and drove to Hayden. He parked down the block and around the corner from his destination. As he walked toward his girlfriend's house, he cast his eyes about the neighborhood to make sure Officer Kelly wasn't close at hand. He text Hannah as he neared her house.

Hannah met him on the front porch wearing her pink sweat pants and a t-shirt.

"Hi Baby," he greeted as he wrapped a soft hug around her.

"I'm so happy to see you." Her manner seemed softer than that of her typical self. "I can't believe my mom took my cell phone and car keys from me for the whole weekend. I missed you so much."

Travis sensed her grief, then unveiled a frown. "Why does she have to be so mean?"

"She says she's just trying to protect me. Figure that one out."

They stepped inside and sat onto the sofa. There was odd silence.

"How are you feeling?"

She kept silent for another moment as she lowered her head. "Empty. Our baby." A tear rolled down her cheek. "Our baby is gone." Hannah rested her head upon Travis' shoulder.

Travis sat idle holding her hand. They didn't talk for some time. During their silence, only the sound of the clock could be heard ticking, then it chimed.

"Are you hungry?" he asked her.

The bounty hunters arrived in the city. Nathan who was driving, took the Sherman exit and pressed toward the city center.

William closed the slider on his cell phone. "Swade said Brett's phone is disconnected."

"That's okay," Saul stated, "We'll just show up at his house and drag him out by his ears."

"Nice illustration there Saul," William cracked.

"I thought so too," he replied with a smile.

William glanced at the GPS, then at Nathan. "You're going to take a left on Eleventh, then a right on Mullan Avenue."

Nathan maneuvered through the two blocks and soon he was upon the house of interest. As he drove by the lot, William spied the property. He made a u-turn at the next block and headed back.

"Everyone ready?" William pressed into action as he unlatched his seat belt. "Saul, I want you to go around back, Nathan will take the front porch with me and I'll secure the door."

Nathan pulled up to the house and as soon as he braked, Saul was out the door and running. Nathan cut the engine and hastened to his position as well, then William knocked at the exterior door. He was taken by surprise when an attractive woman with golden hair opened the door.

She waited for them to speak.

"I'm looking for Brett Willoughby."

"He's not here." She was soft spoken.

He observed her age and presumed she wasn't old enough to be his mother. "Who are you to Brett?"

"His sister. And again, he's not here."

"Can I come in and search?" he presented himself boldly.

"Okay, but be quiet. I have other tenants that I don't want bothered."

"Oh absolutely." Before William could move toward the door, a man came up behind the woman from inside the house.

"What does this guy want?" the man asked the lady in a rough manner.

"He's looking for Brett."

Nathan stepped closer to the door to assist his team leader.

The man sent a glare to both agents. "He's not here."

"That's what his sister just said, now if you'll excuse me, she gave us permission to come in and search."

"No you're not! Our mother is sleeping."

He paused in thought. "So Brett's your brother too?"

The man tightened his lips, not wanting to answer.

William looked straight into his eyes. "Where's your brother at?" His voice had built with intensity.

"I don't have to tell you anything," he shot back.

He took a step forward. "Step aside asshole or you'll be going to jail for interfering or harboring a fugitive."

Nathan had his taser ready to go.

"This is bullshit!" the brother protested, yet he stepped aside. "What gives you the right?"

"We have a warrant for his arrest so that gives us every right!" William radioed to Saul that they were entering the premises, for him to stay in position. He then turned to the woman. "Show me where your mother is sleeping." He had a suspicion.

The two agents followed her into the house and through the living room. She pointed to the far door at the end of the hallway. "That one." She walked back into the living room.

William and Nathan crept down the hallway; William with his pistol drawn. They stopped and stood at the frame of the door. Nathan had William's back as he gave a light tap and listened. He turned the knob and inched the door inward, then with much caution, he peeked in. He thrust the door open. "This isn't mother's bedroom!" he roared as he stepped in. "Brett? Come on out!"

They cast their eyes about the room, noting the twin bed which bore only one pillow and a blanket. They saw mens clothing strewn about the floor and when William looked in the closet, he detected more mens ware.

Nathan glanced at the night table and beheld fragments of marijuana along with miscellaneous items, empty soda cans, and an ashtray full of cigarette butts. "He's been here recently. I can smell him."

Outside, Saul stood guard underneath a cottonwood tree, watching and seeing not one criminal come out the rear door of the house. The birds were chirping and flying from one tree to another. Saul spun his head around when he heard a noise out back by the garage. He radioed to his teammates of it.

"Ten-four." William and Nathan exited Brett's bedroom and quickly searched the remainder of the home. The loud-mouthed man had disappeared from the house while the woman waited at the anterior door. "Where's your brother?" William demanded as he and Nathan neared the door to leave. "He lied to us!"

She shrugged her shoulders.

He knew she had been deceitful as well. "I'm not done with you either.," he snapped at her, then he and Nathan rushed toward the back yard to join Saul for an outdoor search.

She closed, then locked the door. "Well I'm done with you," she spoke to herself, "I let you search." She pulled the shades.

When Saul saw his teammates approaching from alongside the house, he turned and led the way toward the rear part of the large and junky yard. He came upon two steel barrels and lifted the lid of one while Nathan stepped in and raised the other. They were both empty.

William was enroute toward the garage. "One of you go around to the other side," he commanded.

With stealth in his steps, Nathan went in between the tall wooden fence and the building, peeking in through the one small window. He didn't see any movement.

Saul accompanied William around the opposite side of the garage. He stopped near the side door and watched his boss enter in with his pistol aimed forward. "Brett?" William hollered, "Come on out."

When Nathan stepped out from the small gap, the neighbor's dog began to bark. He and Saul both cast their eyes to the open gate, then hurried that way.

In the alleyway, a man had just heaved his leg over the bicycle bar and placed that foot onto the pedal.

"Hey!" Saul roared with his deep voice as he and Nathan hastened to him. "What's your name?"

The fellow was wearing a baggy sweat shirt, the hood was draped around his head as to conceal most of his features. He took a puff of his cigarette. "Who wants to know?"

"I do!" Saul stood at the front of the bike and pushed out his already large chest.

"Jimmy. My name is Jimmy."

He sent him a glare. "You're Brett Willoughby."

"No.. I'm not him I'm Jimmy."

"What are you doing Jimmy – back here in the alleyway?" Nathan intervened.

"I was riding and I dropped my cigarette. I was just getting back on my bike."

William stepped out from the yard and joined the team. He stood near with his arms crossed and watched his new hire handle the matter.

Nathan took hold of his cell phone and brought up Brett's photo. He lifted the device close to Brett's face. "Take off the hood." He and Saul compared his features.

"He has the same eyes and the same tattoo on his neck. It's him." Saul spoke to his comrade, then turned to the fugitive. "You have your ID?"

"No I don't." The man refused Saul's request.

"Get off your bike Brett!"

The fellow was hesitant, but complied.

"You have anything in your pockets that we should know about?"

He was silent.

"Put your hands up." Saul patted him down. "What's this?"

"Protection."

The agent took the piece from within the band of his jeans. "You're a felon. You aren't suppose to be carrying this."

"It's only a toy." He lowered his head in shame.

Saul glanced at it again. "Why would a grown man be carrying a toy?" He tossed the plastic gun to Nathan, then retrieved his handcuffs and bound the fugitive. "Why didn't you go to court?"

He shrugged his shoulders. "Stupidity, I suppose."

William took Brett's bicycle and guided it in through the open gate and set it against the fence. He exited the yard with a shut of the gate and walked with his team and Brett through the alleyway in the direction of their suv.

"I was surprised to see you guys," Brett remarked, "I didn't think Coeur d' Alene had bounty hunters."

Travis left Hannah's house mid afternoon before her younger brother was to arrive home from school. He also wanted to avoid running into her mother. He cast his vision about the neighborhood as he walked the block to his truck.

After he sat onto the driver's seat and keyed the ignition, he looked in his rear view mirror. "Where the hell did he come from?" he spoke of a police car that pulled up behind him with its lights on. He waited for the cop to advance to his door. "At least it's not Kelly this time," he mumbled.

The officer scanned Travis' body as well as the contents on his seat from the angle of which he stood. "We got a call about a suspicious vehicle in the area. What are you doing here?" he asked with a firm tongue.

Travis who prided himself as a reputable bounty hunter, didn't like being on the other end of the questioning. "I'm just visiting a friend."

"Where does your friend live?"

Travis pointed in the direction of Hannah's house.

The officer requested his license and truck registration to verify he had the right person, then asked him to step out of his truck. "It was reported to us that you're seeing a young girl?" he probed as he held his position.

He wore confusion upon his face. "I have a girlfriend, but she's not young like you're suggesting."

"I'll let you explain it to the detective. Turn around and put your hands behind your back. I have a warrant for your arrest."

"On what charge?"

"Lewd conduct with a minor."

He then knew exactly who reported this fabricated crime.

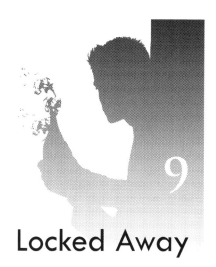

# Locked Away

I t was after dinner when Dominique and Ian left the house to go see Nick's big buy. They hopped into her Ford Explorer and drove to Pinehurst. Upon entering his driveway, they saw an older maroon car parked at the far side of his yard.

"He bought a car?" Dominique imagined as Ian listened.

When they were walking the sidewalk towards Nick's door, he stepped outside.

"Hey Mom. Check out my race car!"

"Awesome. Do I get a space to advertise my books?"

"On the trunk."

She observed the flawless body and rubbed her hand atop of the hard metal.

"I'll have it ready to race in two weeks."

"This will be a good car for you to race in the hobby stocks. You have any sponsors yet?"

\

"I have one other than you and I have one mechanic to help me."

She sent him a tacit expression asking who.

"Well, he's not an official mechanic, but he seems to know a lot about cars. Saul, the new bounty hunter we work with."

"Hmm.." she purred with interest.

Nathan sat onto his bed and flipped through the channels on his television while Felica floated above the foot of his bed.

"I like your mom," she told him, "I can follow her around the house and she don't even know I'm here."

"Yea."

"I saw her folding your clothes that you left piled on the dryer. That was nice of her."

"I get lazy sometimes," he told her, "What about your mom? All you told us was you don't know where she is."

Felica descended and sat onto his chair. "Her name is Paulina and my dad is Eliott."

Nathan pushed the mute button to silence his television.

"My mom was working in a factory and my dad was working for the city, making plans for new streets and sanitation stuff. That's all I remember about their jobs and our house was a fair one."

"People still do that kind of work today. It probably paid good money back then too."

"Maybe, but that wasn't any of my business."

"Do you have any brothers or sisters?"

"No, I was the only child."

"So what did you do?" he asked.

"You mean before I was locked away in my bottle?"

"Yea, when you were a teenager, back in." He had to think.. "1870?"

"Well, it was 1873 when I was fourteen and I was only going to school part of the time. I had to be at home and tend to chores and cook supper every night."

"What did you do for fun?"

"I read."

"Boo.." he lampooned with a grin. "What did you read?"

She gave him a sly glare before she answered. "My favorite book was Uncle Tom's Cabin. It was about slavery. I also liked reading about an Indian girl named Pocahontas. Have you heard of her in this day?"

He chuckled. "Oh yes. They made a cartoon movie about her."

"Aauhh!" she gasped with awe, then she shot herself up into the air and rolled.

Nathan enjoyed her reaction. "Is Pocahontas a real person?"

"Yes. Why wouldn't she be?" Felica replied.

"Because there's a lot of made-up characters these days."

"Oh she's real." She descended and sat again onto his game chair.

He watched her thin pink lips as she spoke of her idol. He wondered what it would be like to kiss a genie.

"She was only twelve years old when she rescued Captain John Smith from being killed by her own tribe."

"She was still a child." he asserted.

Felica nodded. "She helped them to communicate with each other so the white man could survive in the new world."

"That's what the movie says too."

"Does the movie say that when she was seventeen, she was taken hostage aboard a ship and converted to Christianity?"

"I knew she went on a ship."

"She got saved and was baptized. Her new name became Rebecca." She paused as she eyed her rescuer's brother. "Are you saved?"

He was surprised by her question. "Actually, I am," he answered.

"Me too." She felt comforted to know she was among a Christian family. "I asked Jesus into my heart when I was ten."

"I was around six or seven." He thought it was nice they connected in the spirit, yet there was odd silence. "What else did you do or things you like?" he queried.

"I suppose the television and your video games," she answered, "but I'm just taken back at the in-house plumbing and the toilet and the shower and the machines your mom uses to wash and dry clothes," she burst out. "Those are great inventions! And I love how you can turn on the lights. We used candles and lanterns."

"Anything else?" he jested.

She thought. "There's a lot of different material items. You Americans have cars and jets. Is that the correct word, jets?" She glanced into his eyes.

"Jets that fly in the sky."

"Yes." She understood his pun. "Who would of thought that steel ore could fly."

"Or a genie?" He laughed as she smirked. "And don't forget our rockets and spaceships!"

"All we had was the railroad and horse drawn carriage. New York city was just planning and starting to build subway trains." She inhaled, then breathed it out. "People are different too. I am so glad to see that women have more rights and that they can vote."

"Not me."

She sent him a true glare this time.

"Just kidding," he quickly redeemed himself with a smile.

"Okay." She returned the smile. "I did want to say that it's kind of embarrassing for me though that women today dress so.. lightly. We wore dresses, covering our legs and stomachs."

"That is one change I do like!" Nathan asserted.

"It's ungodly."

"Yea, I've heard my mom say that before about bikinis, but she also said there's nothing wrong with showing your knees or lower legs."

"I'm sure I'll get use to some of the new dress codes."

Nathan glanced at his television screen and observed an electronic cigarette commercial being advertised. "I'm curious Felica." He returned his vision to her. "Did a lot of people smoke pot in 1873?"

She moved her head in slow motion back and forth.

"Marijuana?"

"Is that tobacco?" she asked.

"No, but pot is also grown and you smoke it." He paused. "You smoke it to feel good and I heard that the Indians use to smoke it in their peace pipes." He could sense her youth. "Never mind."

"Sorry. I don't mean to be stupid. It's been a long time."

"You're not stupid," he assured her. "I agree that it's been a long time and you're young. I don't even see how you made it in that bottle by yourself for so many years." He reflected on their previous topic. "You could have used some weed."

"If you think so, but it was hard being in that bottle. I cried at times." She bowed her head. "I miss my mom and dad so much."

He thought for a moment. "Can you go see them?"

She looked up at him. "I tried to this past week and nothing has worked. They're locked away or I can only see them by a wish, either by my master's wish or theirs."

"That's tough. Do you think they could still be trapped in their bottle then?"

"Either that or they are dead."

He made a wry face. "Don't say that." There was a pause while he watched his silent actors perform on the television screen. "Why don't we take a drive later and see if we can find another bottle on the beach in the same area where Ian found you? You never know."

"Okay." She sported a half smile. "I'm glad we talked."

"Me too." He was happy to be her friend.

Travis sat onto a worn-out leather cushion atop of a metal chair that had been placed beside a table. He sat within a small soundproof room awaiting the arrival of a detective. He tried to remove the black ink from his fingertips by wiping them onto his jeans.

The door opened. A tall, slender man with a mustache and a five o'clock shadow entered. "Travis.. I'm Detective Johnn. Johnn being my last name spelled with two n's," he spoke slow and firm as he seated himself onto the other metal chair. "Charges were filed against you by the State of Idaho."

"State of Idaho?" Travis questioned while he looked away from the agent who wore a pink shirt and gray slacks. He felt confused within his mind, thinking it was Hannah's mother who was behind this, but then again he thought when he turned back to the detective. "What does the State of Idaho know about my personal life?"

"Enough to file charges." Detective Johnn boast. "You told the arresting officer that you have a girlfriend. What's her name?"

He didn't answer.

"Is her name Hannah?" he probed.

His chair was back away from the table. His torso was now at a forward slant over his lap. He gazed down at the floor.

"Is her name Hannah Stone?" he again asked.

Travis inched a nod.

"You know she's only sixteen."

"She'll be seventeen in three days," his tone carried anger.

"I have to ask you this question. Did you have sexual intercourse with Hannah Stone?"

He was silent for a few moments, then he looked up at the detective. "I'm not saying anything else about this. I have the right to remain silent."

"Then my work here is done." Detective Johnn arose from his chair and left the room.

Travis stood to his feet as well. He paced the floor as he waited for a peace officer to escort him to a cell. A sensation was building inside of him. His breathing became laborious and he began to scratch or rub different places upon himself even though he didn't itch. He craved a cigarette.

The next morning, Travis plead not guilty and was released on his own recognizance. There was a brief mention of a restraining order and after he left the building, he text Hannah. With no immediate response from her, he remembered it was her first day of school as a senior. He stuffed a cigarette in between his lips and started out on a two mile trek to retrieve his truck.

Two hours later, he was back in Kellogg at his apartment. He took a shower, then hopped back into his vehicle and drove to the Underdog's office. Feeling uneasy about his arrest, he remained sitting in his truck with a smoke while he stared at the entrance door. He pondered on how William would react to the charge of lewd conduct with a minor as well as the reputation of the company. He wondered if he'd lose his job.

His cell phone rang. He answered it after recognizing the number. "Hey Baby. I tried to call you earlier, then I remembered you were in school."

"I am. I'm just in between classes right now so I thought I'd call you back real quick."

"I wanted to let you know that after I left your house yesterday, I was arrested."

"What?" Her tone was low, yet her voice rang of dismay.

"I thought you said your mom wasn't going to press any charges?" he challenged.

"I didn't think she was. I'll talk to her tonight and see what she says, then I'll let you know." There was a pause. "Okay?"

"It won't make any difference what she says."

"Other than that, how are you Babe?"

"I'm tired and I still have to go in and talk to William about this, then I'm gonna go home and take a nap."

"The bell's about to ring so I gotta get going. Love you."

"I love you too Hannah."

Afternoon came and Nathan was bored. There hadn't been any work come in from the Underdog's office so he was trying to find things to do. He didn't have a girlfriend and his best friend Sandy had moved away. He already smoked some pot and swam in the family's indoor pool. His younger brother was in school and he was tired of playing video games.

He walked through the living room, past his mother's movie shelf and remembered Pocahontas. He took hold of the two cases and hastened up the stairway to Ian's bedroom. "Hey Felica? I have something for you." He had both movies hidden behind his back.

She appeared in front of him with a smile.

He withdrew the movies and gave them to her.

"Oh.. wonderful!" she exclaimed, then stepped forward and hugged him.

"I'll even watch them with you," he offered. He couldn't believe he was that bored to do so.

Travis had taken his nap and was in the midst of cooking himself some Kraft macaroni and cheese when his cell phone rang. "So what did your mom say?" he asked after they greeted each other.

"She said she didn't press the charges."

"I bet she's lying."

"I don't know. She told me she had talked to the prosecutor about it, then after the abortion she let him know she didn't want to press the charge, but then the state took over. She said once the state takes over there was nothing she could do about it."

"So she did initiate it. Why'd she have to open her big mouth in the first place?"

"I don't know Babe. I know she's friends with him and they were probably talking off the record."

"Just my luck," he replied, then paused. "You know that if I'm found guilty, I'll have to register as a sex offender. That's what William was telling me."

"That sux," she sympathized, but really didn't perceive the significance of it. "Do you still have your job?"

"Yea."

# A New Direction

William called a team meeting at the office. Nathan and Travis sat on the sofa while Saul sat in the clients' chair at William's desk.

"I have an announcement," William spoke from his side of the desk. "We are expanding. It will bring in more work for us all. We are now called The Underdog Bounty Hunters and Investigations." He grinned with pride while he looked at the agents.

"Awesome!" one remarked.

"Our firm is now licensed to do the investigations with Saul and I being the only two to have our PI certificates and badges. Travis and Nathan. You might consider taking the course to get yours. It costs around fifteen hundred."

"Yea, I can do that," Nathan claimed while Travis agreed. "When I win the lottery!"

William and Saul chuckled. "You come up with half and the firm will pay the other half," William told them.

"That sounds fair," Saul encouraged.

"On another note," William continued, "I purchased new t-shirts for us, but if you're working undercover, don't wear them." He lifted a box from the floor and placed it atop of his desk. He withdrew the navy blue t-shirts and passed them out.

"When do we work?" Nathan asked as he took hold of his two shirts.

"Maybe tonight. I have a meeting with our first client here in." He looked at the clock on the wall. "About a half an hour, so I'll need you two to scatter and I'll give you guys a call later."

A young petite woman walked into the Underdog's office carrying a baby carrier. Her countenance bore uncertainty as she approached William's desk.

"Hi. You must be Autumn?" William greeted as he arose to his feet, then reached out to shake her hand.

She responded with a yes.

"I'm William and this is Saul. Please, have a seat."

"You're the investigators?" she inquired as she sat.

William nodded.

She glanced at Saul.

"Boy or girl?" Saul asked to help her feel at ease.

"Boy. His name is Tran."

William had his note pad and pen ready to jot down the details. "You want our help with a custody case, is that right?"

"Yes. My husband Bradford filed for divorce."

William wrote her husband and son's names on his pad.

"And he wants full custody of Tran. He says I'm an unfit mother."

"Do you think you are?"

"Far from it. Bradford's just an arrogant lying pig. Him and his mother."

"Why do you say that?"

"He says things about me that's not true, in particular to his mom, then she spreads it around within the family."

"He said, she said. It's just unproven words," William pointed out.

She thought for a moment. "I'm scared of him. I need you to prove that HE'S the unfit one."

"How's he unfit?" Saul asked this time around.

"He has a temper," she claimed, "especially when he's been drinking. One time when I was driving down the highway, Tran was crying and wouldn't quit crying. Bradford threatened to throw him out the window if I didn't make him stop."

"How'd that turn out?"

"We were almost home."

"He doesn't sound like a nice person. Is he abusive or have you ever had to file for an order of protection?"

"No on the last one."

William frowned. "We need something more.. Maybe an illegal activity?"

She hesitated. "Sometimes he deals."

"Are you two still together or living separate?"

"We're separated."

"Okay Autumn, we'll get on it." William collected a few more details as well as the advancement of his fee, then informed his client that he'd be in touch.

The two investigators got to work immediately employing multiple websites. They were able to pull an elaborate background check on Bradford as well as Autumn. They discovered he indeed had drug convictions of yesteryear as well as theft. They also obtained information of past jobs.

"He's a chemist," William stated to Saul.

"Why would he need to deal then? A chemist makes good money."

"I don't know." He returned his vision onto the computer screen. "He's worked at Crody's Chemical in Coeur d' Alene and Acres Plant Food Center."

"There's a good chance that he's cooking then selling it," Saul presumed.

"And after a little investigating, we'll just see if that's true." He turned to Saul. "It's time to put our surveillance team on him. I want you to train our young agents. Start them out on spying and tailing."

The doors had been locked and the shades were drawn. His black Volkswagon Jetta was parked in the driveway underneath a carport. Bradford stood within his kitchen inside his house, talking on his cell phone with a person he feared. "I'll have your money to you tomorrow, guaranteed."

"You had better have it tomorrow," the caller threatened, "Or else you'll have one less finger to count."

Bradford ended the call and returned to his work. Within his kitchen, he had all his extraction equipment set in place, more specifically the stainless steel rods from the vats that had been shredded into steel wool.

During the long process, he ran the steel material through multiple tubes, using a special formula to flush the sludge out. He then pushed the mud mixings which contained fine dirt powder and solution through the filter where the gold particles separated from the liquid and was recovered.

After a long couple of days, he had himself a small pile of gold. "This ought to take care of that thug," he spoke with relief while he ogled over his collection. "All I have to do now is melt these."

"Well this is boring," Nathan said of their spying operation as he tried to stretch his body from the rear seat of the suv.

Saul glanced back at his trainee. "It can be, but when you finally get results, it's worth the wait."

"It's been three hours and nothing – no traffic."

"He did peek out the window!" Travis added in jest. "He's up to something."

"This stuff will put me to sleep," Nathan continued, "I'd rather be bounty hunting. At least we'd be able to go bang on the door and take someone down!"

"Patience Nathan. You have to have patience for this type of work."

Soon enough, Bradford's front door to his house opened and he stepped out. Without looking about the neighborhood, he walked directly to his car and jumped in.

"Here we go boys." Saul turned the key and started the engine.

"Why don't you let me get out and I'll go snoop around," Nathan suggested as he grabbed the door handle.

"Only if you call William for backup."

"I will." He hopped out and watched Saul speed off. He lit himself a cigarette and called William to let him know of their slight change of plans.

Saul kept his distance as he followed Bradford through Kellogg and onto the freeway. "I hope he's not heading to Coeur d' Alene."

Within five minutes, the pursuit led them past the small town of Pinehurst. "It looks like he IS heading to the city." Saul took hold of his cell phone and called William to inform him of their mysterious trip. He also asked if Nathan called him.

Ian was lying on his bed moaning and groaning, holding onto his abdomen while his mother felt his forehead.

"You're not hot," she spoke of his sickness.

"My stomach hurts."

"What did you eat for lunch today?" She moved his school books aside so she could sit at the foot of his bed.

"Chili and crackers... and a cinnamon roll."

"Yum." She thought for a moment. "You probably have gas and just need to fart."

He knew his genie was listening and he felt embarrassed. He didn't want to pass the stink in front of her. "Do you have any medicine that would help me?"

"Maybe."

Ian kicked his shoes off and climbed underneath his blankets. He turned to his side, keeping hold of his abdomen. Soon he was squeezing out small drifts of soundless air. "Felica?" he called out in a whisper.

She appeared. "What do you want?"

He wanted to see exactly where she was. "Will you open my window?"

"Sure.. it kind of smells in here." She gave him a wink.

"Ohh.." He buried his rosy colored face into his pillow and pushed out another silent fart. When the air cleared, he took hold of the tv remote from his nightstand and turned on his tv. He set the volume a bit higher than usual.

Dominique returned into the room with a fizzy drink for her suffering son, then left. "It's too stinky in here. I'll come check on you in a while."

Ian drank on the remedy as he watched a commercial on the sports channel. "Those are awesome shoes," he managed to say. "I wish I had a pair!" Before he could take back his words, there appeared on his bed, a pair of black and red Nike sneakers. He leaned forward and swooped them up for a closer look. "Oh no. Was that my second wish?" He cast his sights toward his now invisible genie for confirmation.

"You said wish," her reply echoed within his bedroom.

Nathan smoked only half of a cigarette before he butted it and crossed the street. As he advanced, he spied the neighbors to see if anyone was watching. He entered and walked atop of the cement driveway to the side of Bradford's house, then glanced at the windows and observed the shades to be drawn. At the rear of the house, he came upon two garbage cans. He stopped and lifted the first lid. It was empty. The second can contained trash so he set the lid on the other can and ripped the top bag enough to pick through. He didn't see anything that would tie Bradford in with the drug scene. He then heard a vehicle come to a stop out on the street. When he cast his eyes in that direction, he saw that a black suv had parked and he noticed William was waving him over.

The two bounty hunters exited the freeway and followed the black Volkswagon Jetta north on Highway 95 to a side street, then into a parking lot of a mini strip mall.

Bradford parked in front of a store that bought and sold old and rare coins and minerals.

Saul parked two spaces over from Bradford. He and Travis stepped from their vehicle and went into the same business posing as customers.

When Saul entered the store, he saw Bradford talking to the clerk at the counter. He signaled for Travis to browse the coins while he casually, but quickly made his way within ear reach of their accused.

"Are you sure the manager isn't in?" Bradford asked the new clerk.

"No, he's out. You'll have to deal with me today."

He didn't have a choice so he showed her his mass of gold.

"Pretty. Where did you get this?" she inquired.

"I'm a self made gold panner. I have a claim up the North Fork. The manager knows this."

The shop attendant eyed the nugget with her special lens. "I've seen this type of gold before and I don't think it's from your location."

"Excuse me?" Bradford was stunned by her accusation. "It's probably similar to someone else up the North Fork."

"Maybe. However, I am an alchemist and I specialize in metals, especially gold. I can determine its purity and its origin."

"Okay.. The manager has bought my gold before."

The saleslady set his nugget stop of the glass counter top on a napkin. "What's your name? I'll look you up."

Saul glanced aside at the exposed yellow rock, then returned his focus to the minerals underneath the glass. He slowly stepped over to Travis and was inconspicuous in his talk. "I think he's dealing in stolen gold instead of drugs."

"Yea?" he whispered.

"I'm gonna have words with the clerk after he leaves." The agents continued to browse.

Within the next ten minutes, Bradford left the building with cash in hand. The two men watched him through the windows and observed him as he sat in his car and drove away.

Saul advanced to the counter and introduced himself to the clerk with a show of his badge. He gave her a brief explanation of why he was there. "I overheard some of your conversation. Could you tell me who's gold you think this is?" He pointed to the small envelope that she had put it in.

She studied his eyes with a moment of silence. "Crody Chemical."

His eyes widened because of her answer. He knew he was onto something. "When will your manager be in?"

"Tomorrow morning and his name is Jim."

The next morning, Saul met with William back at the Underdog's office where he talked over yesterday's happenings. "I think we need to call Crody Chemical before we go and visit with Jim," he suggested.

"I agree." William took to his laptop to look up the company's phone number for him.

Saul dialed and waited for someone to answer. He was soon transferred to the general manager of Crody. He identified himself as an investigator and they conversed some.

"We had a recent theft here at our company," the manager revealed, "Some of our gold shavings have disappeared."

"Is that all that's missing?"

"Two bottles of our special solution are gone too."

"I know who did it," Saul claimed, then submitted Bradford's name.

The manager confided with him of Bradford's employment and recent dismissal.

"All I need to know is what you want to do about it?" Saul queried.

"I want him thrown in jail, of course!"

"Okay, but if he's thrown in jail after we do get the proof, chances are you'll never see your money back from this."

"That's fine. It will be worth it just to see him locked up."

"I'll be in touch." He ended the call, then cast his attention to William. "He's offered to help finance our quest in retrieving proof."

"I kind of figured that when I overheard you talking."

"Yea," Saul replied with a smile.

William had Travis and Nathan come into the office. "I'm sending you two on another stakeout at Bradford's. Keep a log on the traffic and take photos of all his visitors..inconspicuously." He looked at Nathan. "It may be another long and boring day, but it's work."

"I do appreciate it," he replied, knowing he needed the cash. He and Travis gathered their equipment and left.

After refreshing their mugs with coffee, William and Saul also left, but it was for Coeur d' Alene. Forty minutes of driving, then they exited the freeway and drove to the coin shop.

Upon entering the establishment, they were greeted by a friendly gentleman who turned out to be Jim. They introduced themselves, then as the conversation became more of Bradford and his gold, Jim was less helpful.

"Could I see your records of what he sold to you?"

"I'm not showing you anything!" he thundered.

"Okay, no problem, but let me tell you what's going to happen." William went on the attack. "He stole that gold from Crody Chemical and when I get proof and I will, I'm coming after you for receiving stolen property."

Jim's jaw became stiff and he was silent as he thought on William's threat. "All right. I'll show you his records."

The two investigators looked over the entries on his computer while Jim helped another customer. "According to this data," William spoke to his partner without turning his head, "Bradford has sold over seven thousand dollars worth of gold to him during the past two months."

"That's a felony."

William needed to impress one last detail into Jim's mind before leaving. He waited for the customer to leave, then he took a step toward him. "Here's the deal." He gave him the evil eye. "I need you to keep quiet about this, especially to Bradford. If he finds out we were here, I'll make sure you're standing right next to him when he goes to jail!"

"No, I wouldn't do that. You have my word," he reluctantly agreed.

Both William and Saul shook Jim's twitching hand as they said good bye and left the store with a print-out of Bradford's sales.

"Now onto the next phase."

"Not yet," William cut in. "I received a text to meet up with Swade. He has a bounty for us."

Saul listened as he walked to the passenger's side of the suv.

"We'll just pick up the info on it today and get on it tomorrow."

Later that day, Nathan and Travis met up with William and Saul at the Underdog's office. "We don't have much," Travis highlighted, "At 10:07 this morning, he had two visitors, both men."

"One was a rather buffed guy," Nathan added.

"And that's all the activity there was." Travis concluded as he worked fast to transfer the five photos he snapped from the camera to the computer for everyone's view.

"You did good," William praised. "Now I need you two bounty hunters to go home and get some rest. We have a long day tomorrow. See you at eight a.m."

"And don't forget to eat your wheaties!" Saul sported as he watch them exit the building.

"Ready to make a phone call?" William gestured for Saul to join him at his desk.

The two private eyes sat at close range with their recorder and microphone placed next to the telephone. William turned the device on and glanced at Saul. He then dialed Bradford's home phone number, pressed the speaker button to on, and waited.

"Hello?" A man answered.

"Bradford?"

"Who wants to know?"

"I'm William Hoffman. I'm gonna come straight to the point. I'm a private investigator in Northern Idaho and I'm calling to discuss."

"Wait! Let me guess? Autumn is having you investigate me?"

"No!" He shot back. "I'm calling to discuss an issue that came about from your last place of employment – Crody Chemical."

He was silent.

"Don't you hang up! You worked there, agree?"

"Yea.." he hesitated.

"Crody is missing some expensive steel material from their warehouse." There was more silence as William waited to see what his reply would be.

"What does that have to do with me?" Bradford finally questioned.

"Gold from those mixings are starting to show up in your name as the person who sold those nuggets."

"I have a claim up the North fork where I get my gold."

"Not this time pal!" He held firm. "Not according to the coin shop."

"I think I want to talk to my lawyer before this goes any farther."

"That's probably a good idea," William blurted out, "but before you do, let me tell you I have proof that you stole from them and it's well within the felony range." He could hear Bradford breathing.

"It's only circumstantial."

"I'm going to the Sheriff's office first thing tomorrow with what I have and they in turn are going to arrest you then you can get your lawyer to attempt his magic."

"What do you want from me?"

"To come clean. You owe Crody a lump sum."

"I'm going through a divorce and custody, I can't afford to go to jail."

"It's your choice." He hoped Bradford would take the bait he just threw in front of him.

"Okay," he hesitated, "I may have taken some steel wool from Crody Chemical. Is that what you wanted to hear?"

"The wool that had the gold particles?"

"Perhaps."

William and Saul high fived each other. "Bradford. The one who drives a black Jetta. That was what I needed to hear and I'll let you know what Crody wants to do about it."

"What do you mean – do about it?" he spoke with more boldness. "You just said there will be no record of our conversation which I took as no arrest?"

"I had to get a confession somehow. That was my part," William revealed.

"You think you're slick.. It's my word against your word anyways."

The agents chuckled. "I have your confession on tape."

"You can't record me without my consent!"

"Yes I can. It's all legal. Now calm down, I'll talk to Crody on your behalf and I'll get a hold of you tomorrow."

# In The Cemetery

William started his morning off with a telephone call to Nick, asking if he could help on a bounty, then he called his client. "Autumn, could you pop into my office this morning for an update, that would be great." He left that message on her voicemail.

The Underdogs showed up for work right after eight dressed in uniform. Some filled their mugs with coffee and headed toward the conference table.

William stepped to his crew and began to speak. "Okay men. Here's the story. Swade tried for several days to get a hold of our next fugitive Zachery Reed. With no luck, he finally contacted his co-signer and she told our bail bondsman that he moved to St. Maries."

"That's a violation in itself," Saul added.

"So guess where you're going?" William handed Travis and Nathan each a photo of Zachery. "I'm staying in Kellogg today. That's why Nick is here to take my place."

The four bounty hunters geared up, then left Kellogg in one suv. Saul rode in the back seat with Travis while Nathan sat shotgun and Nick drove.

On the road, Saul went through the file and reviewed Zachery's profile. "He's five feet ten inches, weighs a hundred and seventy. He has a tattoo of a pistol on the side of his neck."

"It's a cool tat." Nathan and Travis both agreed as they recalled the two inch by one inch pistol from his mugshot.

Nick cruised the winding highway through parts of the Panhandle forest, by- passing the town of Harrison, then onward to their destination, traveling parallel with the St. Joe River.

Saul's cell phone echoed the sound of a heavy metal song. He answered and spoke briefly to William, making it a quick call. "We have Zach's cell number now." He leaned forward. "Nick, pull over at the next inlet." He returned to the backrest and turned aside toward Travis. "I'll let you call Zach and tell him you work for Quest Bail Bonds. Tell him to you need him to sign a paper."

"Got it!" he replied.

Around the next bend, Nick slowed and maneuvered the explorer into a small inlet, then parked.

Travis stepped out of the suv with his cell phone because he preferred to work alone when it came to talking on the phone. He lit himself a cigarette, then pressed the seven digit number on his keypad and waited.

Zachery answered his cell phone.

Travis introduced himself as a new bail bondsman and was brief as he explained his call. "I was looking over your file and I noticed you forgot to sign the last page of your application."

"I don't think I forgot," Zach replied.

"I need to met up with you for this signature."

"I remember signing it," Zachery insisted.

"This ain't negotiable. Where can we meet?" Travis sensed he was losing their fugitive.

"You sign it for me and I'll say I signed it."

Travis drew his brow together. "It don't word that way."

"I'm too busy right now. I'll call you later."

"That bastard." Travis cursed under his breath when Zach ended the call. Without hesitation, he pressed the send button for a redial. He waited for Zachery to answer, but instead he was taken to voicemail. "It would be wise of you to give me a call back, immediately!" He roared into his phone.

Saul stepped out of the suv and as he advanced to Travis, he overheard the last of his message to Zach.

Travis glanced at Saul. "He hung up on me and now he won't answer his phone."

The two agents returned and sat inside the suv for further discussion while Nick drove on.

"This guy knows we're after him now," Travis remarked. "He'll be lookin' over his shoulder."

Saul opened Zachery's file. "It says here that he works for Lion's Construction in Coeur d' Alene. My bet is that company is working on a job over in these parts."

Nick accelerated across the bridge and came upon the small city of St. Maries. He pulled into a parking lot adjoined to a gas station and stopped at the far side next to a chain-link fence.

"I'm going inside to see if they know of any construction sites happening around here." Saul stepped out of the explorer.

"Good idea. I'll come with you." Nathan followed him into the convenience store and while he looked for a snack to buy, Saul addressed the clerk.

The man behind the counter responded, "I know there is two or three log houses being built on the outskirts of town. Just take Main Street through town, go past the cemetery and there will be a dirt lane to your left."

"Thank you sir." Saul stepped outside and as he headed across the lot to the truck, he decided to give Zach a call, yet he was taken to voicemail.

Inside the suv, Travis sat with the laptop upon his lap. "There's one construction company here in St. Maries. It might be worth checking into before we go storming out of town on a hearsay."

"If we go in as bounty hunters and Zach works for them, but he's not there, they could alert him we're in town."

"No worries. I'll go in and ask for a job," Nick volunteered. "I'll try to collect some information for you all."

"That may work," one said.

The team yielded to the GPS as it took them through four blocks before arriving at St. Maries Construction. Nick exited the vehicle and walked the distance of two small lots to the anterior door of the building. Upon entering, he greeted the receptionist, then asked about employment.

"I'll give you an application, then you can talk to Tim about it," she replied.

"Is there a lot of construction going on in this area?"

"Some, but he does go out of town quite a bit."

Great.. Nick thought to himself with sarcasm as he glanced down at the application, then after a quick thought, he looked up at the woman. "Is Tim in town today?" Within his mind, he meant is Zach in town with him.

"Yes, however, he only does his interviews in his office."

Nick didn't say anything more, but waved and left the small room. He walked to the explorer and opened the door. "The receptionist said the owner is in town today so Zach could be at the log houses," he informed his teammates of a possible quick catch as he hopped onto the driver's seat in the suv.

"Did you ask about Zach?"

"No.. I didn't want to blow my cover."

There was silence.

"I have an idea." Saul noted the company's telephone number from Nick's application, then dialed it in his phone. "Hello?" he began to speak. "I'm hoping you can give one of your employees a message for me; Zachery Reed? I'm his neighbor and I need him to call me asap. Can you get this message to him?"

"Why don't you just call his cell phone and leave a voicemail?" the receptionist queried.

"I have. He's not answering and it's about his dog so I thought it to be an emergency."

"I'm not saying anything about any employees, sorry." She ended the call.

Saul wore shock upon his face. "She hung up on me."

"It happened to me too."

Nick started the engine and proceeded out of the parking lot. He headed back toward Main Street, turned left and aimed the vehicle for the outskirts of town. When he came upon the cemetery, he slowed.

"I don't like cemeteries," Travis blurted out softly.

Saul had his window rolled down with his head nearly poked out. "Let's scope the place first before we rush in," he recommended to the team as Nick turned onto the dirt lane.

On his computer, William clicked the mouse button to take him to his home page. He was distracted when his client Autumn, entered into the office carrying her baby. His face sported a welcoming grin as she approached his desk and sat. "Thank you for coming in," he said to her.

She cast her wide-open eyes upon him, eager to hear what he had to say.

"Our goal here at Underdog Investigations is to uncover the truth, whether it's gain for our clients or information and mishap against our clients." He paused. "We tailed Bradford for two days. We don't think he's dealing drugs nor do we think he's seeing any other woman. I'm sorry, but as of now, there's nothing to prove that he's unfit unless you use his past arrests." He sat back in his chair as he eyed her. "I need to know what you want to do about this; keep us on his tail for a few more days or I refund some of your money to you now?"

She scratched her head in thought as she looked down at her son Tran.

"I'm not an attorney," he added, "but I would guess that more than likely, you'd get custody. The mother usually does, unless there is something you're not telling me?" He raised a brow.

"No. I'm not hiding anything. Is two days long enough to determine he's not dealing?"

"In this case I would say yes." He figured she didn't need to know of Bradford's theft since he was going to make it right.

"Okay, I'll take the refund and be on my way."

The bounty hunters were parked and sitting within the suv underneath a large cottonwood tree just off the dirt lane. Nathan who rode shotgun held his binoculars to his eyes, spying the log houses.

Saul stepped out of the explorer and used his a second pair of binoculars to get a better look at the construction site. He observed the roofers atop of the two roofs as well as their two trucks and the trucks that belonged to St. Maries Construction. He noted where the dirt road curved around the cemetery and alongside the hill. "They'll see us coming for sure," Saul spoke to the three agents through the open windows.

"Maybe so, but they won't know we're bounty hunters until we step out of the vehicle with our hardware," Travis stated. "Then it will be more difficult for Zachery to run."

"But not hide," Nick asserted.

"He can hide up on the hillside if he's fast enough."

There was a moment of silence then Saul spoke. "I say Travis and Nathan head out on foot through the cemetery."

"What?" Travis questioned with quick turn of the head.

The team chuckled.

"It's daylight! What could happen?" Saul encouraged to him.

"Creepy things!"

Again the team laughed.

Travis gave the evil eye, then he and Nathan jumped out of the explorer. He lit a cigarette and walked around the vehicle to join his teammate. He observed two black crows cawing and flying above, finally landing on two separate headstones. "What's that shit?" He glanced at his brother.

Nathan smiled while they crossed the dirt lane. Both bounty hunters hopped the small picket fence and headed toward the log houses.

Saul had seated himself in the passenger's seat of the suv. "We'll wait until they get closer to the houses before we take off," he told Nick.

Travis and Nathan tried to step carefully between the graves and headstones. "You know we're still walking on dead people."

"Hey.." Nathan pointed to a gravestone. "That man has your last name!"

"No he don't. Stop it!"

"Maybe he's your great great uncle?"

Travis looked on the headstone at the dates. "He lived ninty-one years. That's a long time."

As they continued on their way, they noticed the brightness from the sun had suddenly vanished. They cast their eyes to the sky and saw a huge puffy black cloud moving in, followed by a mass of gray.

"Really?" Travis jested, "It's trying to spook us while we're in the cemetery."

"Let's just focus in on getting our fugitive now before it rains."

Within the dim vicinity, the agents crept and ducked behind the tall headstones and bushes. When they reached the other side of the yard, they stopped and stood atop of a wide rock underneath a pine tree. Travis radioed to Saul of their position. "We're looking for him now. Over." He held his binoculars to his eyes.

"Ten four. Nick and I are heading out at a slow pace," Saul replied.

Travis moved his focus to the roofers then along the background of the dense forest. "I can't tell who's who."

Nathan flinched backward, unaware he dropped his binoculars. He peered to his right then gasped. "I just saw a shadow dash by."

Travis spun his way and scanned the passage. "Just like the one I saw underground, huh?" he expressed with eagerness.

"You saw it too?" Nathan probed.

"Not this one." He noticed an eerie cast upon his brother's face. "We've both seen ghosts."

"Let's get out of here. This is not where I want to be." Nathan bent down and took hold of his binoculars. With no one paying mind to them, he radioed to Saul as they walked with no visible weapons toward the log structures.

Nick accelerated and drove the gravel lane. When he neared the construction site, both he and Saul observed the rookies to be stepping into the first structure. He stopped the suv at the second log frame and parked.

"Let's go!" Saul jumped out and hastened in through the construction of everything, scanning the faces of the workers as he made his way to the rear.

Travis and Nathan found no one that resembled Zachery. As they walked toward the third structure at the far side of the lot, they took note of the three men that were lounging about on a bench at the edge of the cemetery lawn.

"There wasn't anyone over there when we came rushing through a minute ago," Nathan recalled.

"Let's go check em' out." The two bounty hunters advanced toward the men who were eating their lunches or smoking a cigarette. Travis and Nathan were aware that their comrades had entered the cemetery some twenty feet away and was creeping around bushes and headstones to come up behind the workers.

The agents stopped ten feet from the men. "Zachery Reed?" Travis demanded as he looked at the guy with the tattoo of a pistol on his neck. "We have a warrant for you."

Zach wore a glare within his sights. "What are you guys doing by coming to my work?" He arose to his feet.

Saul and Nick stood as back-up for their teammates if their fugitive wanted to turn and run.

"You should of met up with me somewhere."

"Where's the paper you need me to sign?"

Nathan advanced closer to him. "You need to turn around and put your hands behind your back!" He commanded while he went for his handcuffs.

"No," the fugitive replied, then pushed on Nathan's chest, daring him to make a move.

Travis showed Zach a taser gun. "Now!" he ordered.

The fugitive considered his weak threat and wanted to resist, however, he slowly raised his arms and moved them to his backside. "Only because I value my job."

"You need to value your bail bondsman too," Nathan spoke while he cuffed him.

# A Second Contact

Nathan slept until ten a.m. He was awaken when Felica slid the window open, causing the warm breeze to whistle in as it blew the thin curtain back into the room. "It's nice outside.... The sun is shining," she spoke of the day, "We should go somewhere before your boss calls you in."

Nathan moaned as he stretched within his bed, then he popped an eye open and saw the curtain flapping. He glanced at Felica and noticed her latest up-to-date outfit. "Where are you getting all your clothes?"

"From the catalogs I obtained."

He lifted his head once again for a peek.

"When I see an outfit I like, I snap my fingers and wish, then one appears before me in my size."

"In your size?" he teased, "How convenient." He stared at her with a near smile as he sat up to the edge of his bed. "Isn't that stealing?"

"Not if I snap it back to the owners each night, huh?"

He shrugged his shoulders at her, then lit a cigarette. "Where do you want to go today?"

"I'll just hang out with you."

"We could go to the beach?" he suggested.

Nathan's bedroom door sat ajar, but came open. "Did I hear beach?" Ian asked as he poked his head around the door.

"No, I said breach." He glanced at Felica who remained at a float in the air.

"Why would you say breach? You're going to the breach?"

Nathan grinned. "Why were you eavesdropping?"

"I wasn't. I was just looking for my genie."

"And here I am," she added into the conversation.

"Aren't you suppose to be in school?" Nathan queried.

"I have the day off. There's a teacher's meeting."

Travis stood in front of the bathroom mirror, combing the gel through his spiked blond hair. He leaned in and observed a blemish upon his cheek. He squeezed on it, forcing the puss to rocket and splat onto the mirror. "Nice," he spoke aloud, then inspected the inside of his nose. He had a case of the butterflies and not all the flies were stress related, some were angry butterflies. He had tried to prepare himself for whatever questions the examiner may ask by reading two articles on how to pass a polygraph test.

He soon walked out of his apartment and after locking the door, he jumped into his truck and left Kellogg. He drove to Coeur d' Alene and advanced to Government Way. He had ten minutes until his appointment.

He stood at the entrance of the federal building and exhaled. He scanned the wordings on the glass doors as he entered into the foyer and after reading names of the different offices on a board, he headed down a corridor until he reached the correct suite.

Inside the testing room, it was just him and the tester. He sat with his chest and finger strapped with wires.

"It's going to record your blood pressure and your breathing so try not to be nervous," the tester told Travis while he observed the lines on the paper to be at a still. "The machine will pick up on it and register it as a possible flub or lie."

Travis told himself before he had even been strapped in to just breathe regular and act as though the wires weren't there.

The polygraphist glanced at Travis. "Ready?"

"Sure," he answered.

There was odd silence.

"Is today Thursday?" The examiner started with a simple question.

Travis answered yes.

"Are we in Coeur d' Alene, Idaho?"

"Yes."

"Are we sitting in a room full of gorgeous women?"

He wanted to snicker at the tester's quirky question. "No," he replied.

"Do you have a girlfriend?"

He knew it was becoming more serious.

"Do you know a Hannah Stone?"

"Yes I do."

"Just a simple yes or no," the examiner said as he watched the lines on the paper to read of his honesty. "Is it true you've known Hannah Stone for six months?"

"Yes."

"Do you know Hannah is sixteen years of age?"

"Yes." He wanted to explain.

The examiner made a small mark on the paper with his pencil. "Did Hannah tell you she was sixteen when you met?"

He felt some relief in his mind. "No."

The polygraphist drew another mark on the paper. "Did you meet Hannah at the mall?"

Travis answered the man, then he answered two more questions.

"Have you ever kissed Hannah on the lips?"

He responded with a yes.

"It'll get more personal now," the examiner told him.

The room seemed to of become smaller and darker with no windows to the outdoors, just a one way on the wall.

"Did you have sexual intercourse with Hannah Stone?"

He tried to keep his angry butterflies at bay as he replied.

The tester made a mark on the paper. "Did you have intercourse more than once with Hannah?"

"Yes."

"Did you ejaculate inside of Hannah Stone?"

Travis was stunned by the question. "Yea.. that's what happens when you have sex."

The polygraphist groaned with displeasure as he labeled the passage with a particular symbol, then he repeated the question.

Travis responded with only a yes this time because he grew eager to be done with it and leave.

Two questions later and the test was over. When the examiner said good bye, he left the building, aching to smoke a cigarette. As he walked to his truck, he dialed Hannah's cell number.

"Hi Baby!" she answered.

"I feel violated," he joked with his girl. "They asked me way too many questions. Questions that were none of their business."

"Poor baby. I'll have to make it all better later.. okay?"

"Mmm..."

Dominique received a phone call from William asking her to come in. As she dressed herself in her blue jeans and sweet Nike's, she wondered if Saul would be there. A half an hour later, she entered the Underdog's office.

William was posted at his desk while his employee Saul occupied a chair opposite him. "Hey girl." William tilted his head and spoke to her in a spirited manner.

She carried a smile on her face even though she told herself not to. As she approached, she glanced at Saul, this time she had a close-up shot of his brawny frame. She found it hard to listen to William speak.

"This is Saul, our newest fugitive hunter and investigator."

She glanced at William, then cast her curious eyes back to Saul for a longer look. It took her a moment, but she replied hello. "I've heard about you through my sons. It's nice to finally meet you." She held her tongue of the time she cast a secret stare at him from her bedroom window when he stopped by her house with Nathan. He had the passenger's side window down that day and he was puffing on a cigarette. Dominique sat onto a chair and tamed her smile.

Saul turned to her causing their eyes to make a second contact. "You'll be working with me today," he spoke using his smooth deep voice.

"Yea.. I figured so. You and William." She felt a little out of place since she hadn't been out on a bounty in a while even though she knew she was only there to search the female fugitive after she was cuffed.

William printed out three photocopies of their fugitive, Emmy Watson and handed one to Dominique and one to Saul.

The trio agreed to drive to Emmy's last known address since she wasn't answering her telephone or returning the bondsman's calls. Dominique was put into a bullet proof vest before leaving.

They hadn't driven far when they arrived at their destination on Riverside Avenue in Kellogg. Saul exited the suv before it came to a complete stop. He jumped over a short fence, ran alongside and around the house to the back yard where he stood guard beside a maple tree in the center of the expanse.

Dominique advanced with William up the sidewalk to the front porch, noting the closed curtains. They stood at the door frame while William knocked on the pine wood and listened. It didn't take long for the structure to open with a heavy set woman standing within the entry. Inside the living room it appeared dark.

"Hello ma'am," William spoke, "We're here for Emmy Watson."

"I haven't seen her."

"Then you'll have no problem with us coming in to look?"

The woman denied entry.

"This is the address she gave to us when she wanted to be bonded out of jail!" he roared as he cast his sights into the dim space behind the woman and saw a figure peeking from the edge of the wall. "Hey you!" He pointed that way. "Come here!"

The broad woman adjusted her stance at the doorway, acting as a blockade. Dominique being five two and slender, bent down and quickly forced herself in between the door frame and the woman, making it through to the other side. She stepped forward and aimed a small can of pepper spray in the way of an unknown person. "Hands where I can see them!" she demanded, yet inside her person, she was shaking.

William radioed for Saul to assist them up front. With a push to the stout woman, he forced his way past her. When he sprang to Dominique, a different woman was lifting her hands above her shoulders.

"Are you Emmy?" With William at her side, Dominique advanced to and spun their fugitive until she was pressed up against the wall. She took hold of her wrist and cuffed her to the back.

William had the large woman screaming her protests in his other ear, finally turning and ordering her to zip her lip and sit on the nearby couch.

Saul hastened around to the front of the house and rushed through the open doorway. He observed William and Dominique to be controlling the situation so he halted at the couch to make sure the large woman sat.

Dominique took hold of Emmy's arm and walked her outside. William and Saul followed, closing the door behind them. Dominique guided their fugitive to the suv where she patted her down. "Do you have anything on yourself that you don't want to be taking to jail?"

"No.." she replied.

William stepped in. "Good job Dominique." He attended to Emmy. "Why'd you quit calling in? You should of known Swade would send someone out to nab you."

"It's hard to keep up on appointments and paperwork when I don't live in Kootenai County."

Saul stood idle, listening to William and his bounty. He cast a secret eye on Dominique, viewing her posture and liking her figure.

Dominique turned toward the vehicle's door, but before she could lift the handle, Saul quickly reached forward and opened the door for her.

She gave him a quizzical glance, then as she smiled, a tingly sensation rushed through her heart. "Thank you," she spoke softly.

William recuffed Emmy to the front, then directed her to the back seat where Dominique strapped her in.

The large woman exited her house and approached the bounty hunters. "Can I talk to my niece for a moment?"

Emmy cried on her aunt's shoulder.

"Everything will be okay. I'll get you out somehow." She tried to comfort her while she wrapped her with a hug.

Soon the agents left Riverside Avenue and headed back to the office to drop Dominique off. "I'll see you around some other time, I suppose," she cast to Saul and stepped away.

"Definitely!" he answered her.

William called the bondsman to let him know that they nabbed his bounty, then he and Saul drove their fugitive to Coeur d' Alene.

Saul was lost in thought for the first part of the trip back to Kellogg. He cast his sights out his side window and stared at the mountain sides. He peeked over at William who was driving, he hesitated speaking, then he glanced again at him and cleared his throat. "I wanted to ask you about Dominique."

William turned his head toward the agent with a grin.

Saul observed the gaping of William's mouth. "Stop it! I was just wondering what she's like?" he joked with a roar.

William continued to smile broadly. "She's a nice person."

"How nice?"

William threw him an odd look.

"What I mean is that I'm tired of crazy women who act psychotic."

"Dominique's not crazy. She's sweet. She's devoted to her writing and her sons.. and the Lord. I know that much."

"Then she's a happy divorced woman?"

"As far as I can tell, but you never know until you get to know a person. You thinkin' about asking her out?"

"Maybe."

"I knew you were sweet on her."

This time it was Saul who grinned from ear to ear.

"Go ahead and ask her," William urged, "What do you have to lose?"

Nathan, Ian, and Felica arrived at the beach house and parked down by the dock. "It doesn't look like anyone's here," one said as they stepped out of the truck.

Nathan lit himself a cigarette and led the way, taking small steps alongside the beach and upon the dirt trail that zigzagged through the thicket; the same direction he had gone when he followed Ian last week. He stepped on the flat rocks until he saw the array of boulders.

The trio split up. Each went to separate areas among the huge rocks, searching the gaps for any kind of material that would resemble a bottle.

"I found a quarter!" Ian boasted after picking up the coin from atop of the stone mass and showing it.

"Keep looking." Nathan instructed with a smile.

Ian checked around the boulder he was standing on, then jumped to the adjoining rock where Felica stood. He helped to search for glass fragments or anything that shined. "Why are we looking for another bottle anyways?" he probed while he glanced at the genie, then looked to his brother for an answer.

Felica skipped to a second rock before she revealed the answer to him. "To find my parents!"

Ian turned his head and stared at her with a gape. "And you think their bottle could be here at the beach too?"

"Maybe," she replied.

"Can't you just use your power to go see them or bring them here?"

She paused. "Only with a wish."

He cast his vision to the ground and gave thought to his last wish.

Nathan perched himself down on his rock and lit a cigarette while he listened to their silence.

Ian lifted his head and moved his eyes toward Felica. "I'm ready to ask you for my wish."

She smiled, hoping he would give her the wish of reuniting with her parents.

"I wish for three more wishes."

Nathan chuckled. "Yes, bro!"

Felica swallowed the disappointment in her throat as she looked away and sat on the boulder.

Both brothers detected her sorrow. They looked at each other, not knowing exactly what to do. Finally, Nathan gestured with his head for Ian to say something.

Ian cleared his throat. "I want to use my first wish of my three new wishes to send you on a vacation to see your mom and dad."

Nathan arose and leaped onto Felica's boulder. He sat next to her, then after seeing a tear run down her face, he reached over and used his finger to wipe it dry. "Don't cry," he whispered.

"I'm just being very emotional. It's been many years since I've seen my parents."

"I know, but Ian did wish for you to see them." He observed her from the corner of his eye and tried to cheer her up with a tickle to her cheek.

She smiled and waited some five minutes before she granted Ian his wish of three more wishes. Then when she wished to see her parents, a bottle similar to hers, appeared on the boulder next to them.

They all gasped, then stood to their feet. They glanced at each other and stared at the bottle that was covered with gritty matter.

Felica leaped to that rock. "Momma!" She dropped to her knees and grabbed the soiled bottle. She pulled the cork out and waited anxiously for her mom and dad to arise.

# Assault with A
# Deadly Weapon

William and Saul sat at their desks and waited for their next client to arrive for his eight a.m. appointment. William had his laptop open to his e-mails while Saul sipped on a cup of coffee and messed with his tape recorder.

The client soon entered the Underdog's office with his attorney. Everyone greeted each other, then the two men sat in the chairs William had provided for them.

Saul turned on his recorder.

"Mason," William began with a fold of his hands upon his desk. "What can we do for you as investigators?"

The attorney spoke first. "Mason needs evidence that he used his gun in self-defense."

"That may be tough to do." William told them as he observed his client's face to be hairless and smooth as a baby's butt. "How old are you?" He was curious as he veered from the subject.

"Eighteen."

William took a moment to cast a glance at Saul and his squeaky recorder. "Tell me your story Mason. We'll go from there."

"I was arrested for assault with a deadly weapon and malicious harassment. I pulled a gun on my buddy, Tony who happens to be half Haitian and half Hawaiian."

"Malicious harassment is considered to be a hate crime," the attorney interjected, "Just in case you didn't know that." He was eyeing the investigators.

"But that's not why I pulled a gun on him!" Mason claimed as he sat forward in his seat.

"Why do you think your actions were in self-defense?" he asked the young man.

"My friends and I have always pranked each other since sixth grade. After the last prank and words with Tony over the phone, I decided to put an end to all the mischievous acts."

"What was the last prank?"

Mason reclined in his chair. "A cab full of wood kindling in my truck."

William wanted to laugh as he pictured what Mason described as being filled up to the sunroof. "Okay Mason, go back to when you discovered the wood, after you opened the door and got attacked by falling sticks."

"I called Tony cuz I was angry. I called him a mother ...er and told him I was going to kick his ass!"

"What was Tony's reaction to that?"

Mason recalled the conversation as he lived it.

"Yea right," Tony exclaimed into his cell phone towards Mason's threat, "Like you could ever kick my ass!" He taunted with a laugh.

"Who do you think you're screwing with? This ain't funny." Mason had just worked an eight hour afternoon shift and was tired.

"Relax. It was a joke. You know, like the crap you pulled on me out camping?"

"No, it's not a joke this time. Meet me in the back parking lot of the auto parts store at midnight and I'll show you how funny this isn't!"

"You serious?" Tony responded.

"Yea. Show up and you'll see when I kick the shit out of you!"

"That's not going to happen." He inhaled a large breath as he considered his invite. "Fine. I'll see you at midnight."

William jotted down some notes while he stayed alert to his client's story.

Mason glanced at Saul, then at William. "I got to the bar first. I drove my dad's truck."

William gestured with his index finger that he wanted to interrupt. "Because your truck was still full of kindling?"

Saul turned away with a grin plastered upon his face as he imagined the prank again.

The client bowed his head. "That and I knew my dad had a pistol in the glove box. My only thought about the gun was for protection if any emergency came about."

"What happened after you arrived at the bar?"

"I backed into a spot at the edge of the building and waited. A minute later I saw Tony entering into the parking lot with two other vehicles, one I recognized."

Tony steered his truck to a location across the lot, kiddie-corner of Mason and parked with his headlights beaming onto his challenger's passenger door.

Mason froze.

The two vehicles stopped in a circular fashion just feet away, pinning him in. They shut down their headlamps.

Mason began to be concerned as he sat alone. He peered through the darkness and counted more than one head in each car.

After Tony set his truck in park, he reached for the door handle, anticipating Mason would do the same.

Mason rarely walked away from a fight as the loser, however, this wasn't a case of one on one or even three on one; he figured at least five. He realized talking it over wasn't an option tonight, neither was sitting in a locked truck waiting for them to attack in some form. He didn't want to show himself as a chicken either, so with much discretion, he reached with his right hand into the glove box and grabbed the gun.

Tony honked his horn, trying to egg Mason on, then his recruited posse also gave a few short blows.

Mason raised the semi-automatic .45 caliber with handle activated laser sight toward his opponent. He pointed the red beam through the windshield, holding the dot steady on his contender's chest.

"That doesn't sound like self-defense to me," William stated as he lifted a brow to Mason.

"I just wanted to scare him."

He glanced at Saul, then returned his vision onto his client. "Okay continue to tell your account of things."

Jim who sat with Tony in the cab of his truck saw the red beam shining in and quickly pointed it out.

Tony's first reaction was to lean to his side to escape the path of the laser, yet when he moved aside, there was not enough space to maneuver because of the door, nor could he lean to his right or else he'd be in Jim's lap. He didn't think his ex-friend Mason would actually shoot, however, he wasn't going to take that chance. He reached for the key and cranked the engine, then as soon as he had it in gear, he pressed the gas pedal to the floor, creating a quick getaway with the skidding and screeching of tires. Tony blast past his posse, leaving them in the parking lot.

Mason looked up at William who was playing with the edge of his paper. "What did you do after Tony left?" he asked his client.

"I set the pistol on the seat and sped home." He paused. "I parked in the garage and put the caliber back in the glove box then I went into the house and tiptoed to my room."

"Tiptoed?"

Mason smiled.

William thought a moment. "How did it come about that you were arrested?"

The attorney gestured for an interruption. "The police report says the victim. Tony, called 911 and made a complaint that Mason being an old friend from school, had been harassing him and threatened violence to his body when he pulled the gun on him."

"Did you shoot the gun at any time or say anything of his ethnicity?"

"No.. no I didn't. There's no reason why I would say anything about his race." There was a small pocket of silence in which the sound of Mason's breathing could be heard. "Can you prove self-defense?" he asked the investigator.

William sat with the police report at his desk. He wasn't smiling as he scanned it. "It could be tricky. It sounds like a classic case of he said, you said, then we also need to look at the fact that there are witnesses to you aiming the pistol at his chest."

"He brought his gang to ensnare me and kick MY ass!"

William looked to Saul with a confused expression, then cast his attention back to Mason. "You asked him to meet you there so you could kick HIS ass. Of course he's gonna bring back-up!"

"Who's side are you on?" Mason raised himself upward in his chair and glared at William. "I didn't threaten violence on his body when I drew the gun – as he claims," he emphasized, "Nobody saw the gun, it was just the laser they saw."

"Calm down. I am on your side. It just doesn't look good for you right now."

Mason eased back into his chair. He glanced over at his lawyer who returned his quick look.

The investigator cleared his throat. "Do you know any of the names of Tony's posse?"

"I know who was in one vehicle. Lonny and Eva."

"Thank you." He took a drink of his coffee. "Maybe I can put something together." He then quoted his fee.

"Sounds good." Mason felt comforted to hear William's words that he accepted his case, then he endorsed a check to him.

Saul turned off the recorder.

"I'll be in touch." William arose and shook the client's hand and the attorney's hand before closing the meeting. He slipped the check into a folder.

After the two exited the building, William text Travis, asking him to come in for the day.

Saul arose from his chair with his cup in hand and headed to the coffee maker for a refill. As he ambled alongside William's desk, he observed him taking from his top drawer, two mini microphones and their wires.

Twenty minutes later and Travis arrived for work. He was briefed on the case, yet his focus remained on his career choice. He was wrestling with new feelings of anger toward law enforcement and he disliked the fact that his occupation was connected to that. He didn't like the man who tested his capability of lying nor did he like Officer Kelly.

"Let's start out with the pals that helped Tony with the posse just to see how many stories we hear, whether they're different, the same, or close to." William looked at his notes. "Most important, we need facts."

"I agree," Saul stated, "Let's get wired up and go." Saul cast his attention toward his colleague and noticed the blank look upon his face. "Travis?"

Travis broke from his thoughts. "Yea. Let's do this."

William and Saul strapped the mini microphones onto their bodies and with the information and cell phone in hand, they left.

The three investigators motored their way to the crime scene to get a visual of the area, then drove the way Mason said he went home that night. They didn't stop at his house, but continued on to Kator's Kafe' where their first witness Lonny, worked as a cook.

The agents turned on their mini microchip recorders before exiting the suv, then they entered the eatery. William observed the lack of customers as he spied the dining room. Only one gal sat at the counter sipping on a coke.

While the team perched themselves onto three separate stools, the waiter approached and asked them their pleasure.

"We'd like to speak to Lonny."

Within the minute, he came out of the kitchen and stepped around the counter. He sat next to the girl and faced the men, waiting for one to speak.

"We're doing an investigation and I heard you were in one of the vehicles at Tony and Mason's social gathering last week – you and your girlfriend Eva?"

"Yea."

The woman who sat beside Lonny perked up. "I'm Eva."

William smiled at her. "Hi Eva." He returned his sights to Lonny. "We're wanting any information that you may have about this matter."

"A prank gone wrong is what started it," Lonny answered, "I was told Mason got really peeved from it and wanted to kick Tony's ass – threatened him real good."

"How?"

Lonny chuckled. "He said he was going to shove one of those sticks where the sun don't shine."

"That's a bit extreme. So what really happened that night? Weren't these guys pals?"

"Yes. Ever since second grade."

Both witnesses were anxious to tell their own account of that late evening. One would barely get a word out before the other would interrupt with corrections.

The cafe door opened with the sound of a bell. Lonny turned himself around and saw Tony enter in. "Oh shit," he mumbled to himself. While the agents looked on, Lonny stood to his feet and advanced to his pal and whispered, "Those guys are investigators."

Without saying a word, Tony turned and walked out of the restaurant.

Travis looked at William, waiting for him to jump up and go after him.

He observed Travis' expression. "I have another plan that just came to mind. Let's go." He paid for the drinks, then left the cafe with his team. After they stepped outside, Tony was gone.

"That was almost a waste of time," one said.

The Underdogs returned to their office. William sat at his desk and listened to a message that Swade left on their machine. The agents overheard from the speaker and knew they'd be going after a bounty. William moved his eyes to his employees. "I'm calling Nathan in to go with you two so I can get started on obtaining that proof we need for Mason."

Saul raised his brow at William.

"It's time to use some modern technology."

# Up on The Skid Trail

William retrieved the information for their next bounty from the fax machine and stepped to his crew. "He's a rough one. Swade said he almost didn't bail him out," he spoke of Darin Scott as he handed the stack of papers to Saul. "You're in charge of this one, but if you need me, I'm just a phone call away." He sat at his desk with his computer while Saul led Travis and Nathan into the conference room for a briefing.

Saul skimmed through the file. "He's six three and weighs only a hundred and fifty pounds meaning he's just a string bean."

The two agents agreed as they studied his mugshot.

Travis wrote Darin's features upon the marker board as Saul continued. "Blond hair and green eyes. He has two tattoos above his eyebrows – tattoos of swords."

"All our bounties have cool tats. He should be easy to spot out."

"Let's get geared up and go after this fugitive. He's changed his phone number so nobody could get a hold of him and he's skipped out on a 50,000. bond."

William sat alone in the office at his desk typing in vital information for a new facebook account. "Hmm.." he pondered on a name. "Cheyenne," he chose.

After he completed the sign up process, he logged in using his new username and password, then keyed in Tony's first and last names and clicked on search. He tapped his fingertips atop of his desk as he waited a few moments for a profile to appear. "That's my guy!" he boasted to himself when he saw the photo. He studied Tony's information to figure out some of his likes. "Football... The Seahawks." He continued to read out loud. "Car races, American History, pizza. I can work with those."

William began to type out a message. I READ YOUR PROFILE PAGE AND NOTICED YOU ARE INTO AMERICAN HISTORY AND ARE ATTENDING A CLASS AT NORTH IDAHO COLLEGE. I ALSO AM A HISTORY MAJOR AT A DIFFERENT SCHOOL AND MAYBE WE CAN COMPARE NOTES SOMETIME. I'M JUST LOOKING FOR A NEW FRIEND, CHEYENNE. He clicked on send and his first message went through the system. He leaned back in his seat with his arms partially raised above his head and his fingers entwined. "Now I just have to wait for Tony to reply and hopefully it don't take too long." He finished his cup of coffee.

After meeting with Swade just off the Interstate 90 Cataldo exit for the warrant, Travis drove north on the dirt road while Saul navigated using a map. "There's nothing like a malfunctioning GPS," he cracked, "and according to Swade's directions, we're to go five miles until we cross a small wooden bridge, then turn left." He pointed to the area with his fingertip. "This map doesn't show the bridge, but that's okay, we'll still find our way."

Nathan who sat in the back seat, popped his head forward after listening to Saul jabber. "Darin thinks no one is going to come all the way out here in the woods to retrieve his ass."

"But he's wrong!" Saul finished Nathan's sentence in jest.

Travis crossed over the wooden passage and stopped because the road came to a split. "Which one Saul?" he asked.

Saul visually searched for a street sign and observed there to be none at either corner. He scanned the map, then looked up. "Take this one." He suggested the lane that seemed a bit wider.

When Travis approached the first homestead, he slowed so Saul and Nathan could read the name on the mailbox.

"We need to go talk to these people."

Travis steered the vehicle into and up the long driveway. After he parked, his teammates stepped out of the suv and approached the front door of the house, then knocked.

The door opened and a woman holding a rifle appeared. She held her weapon in full view ready to aim and shoot.

"Whoa, whoa!" Saul responded as both he and Nathan stepped backward. "We're bounty hunters."

"What do you want?" she demanded in a composed manner.

"We're just looking for someone. Darin Scott." He showed her his photo. "Do you know him?"

"There's a Bill Scott up at the Scott Ranch. Maybe Darin is his kin."

"Where is this ranch, may I ask?"

"Go back to the fork and take the other road alongside the creek for about a mile or so. You'll pass by a red barn before you turn into his private drive."

"Thank you ma'am."

William was elated when his Cheyenne received a return message with a friend request from Tony saying he could always use another friend, especially if they were female. William immediately accepted the request, then sent him a second message. I'M GLAD TO HEAR BACK FROM YOU. I'M BUSY WORKING ON A PAPER FOR SCHOOL SO I CAN'T CHAT LONG. WHAT ARE YOU UP TO? William wanted to keep it simple.

Within the minute, Tony sent a brief statement. U NO WHAT I LOOK LIKE, BUT I DONT NO WHAT U LOOK LIKE!?

"I think he may be a horndog," William spoke to himself, then began typing in his response. I'LL POST MY PICTURE WHEN I'M DONE WITH MY REPORT. He sent the message.

WHAT U WRITING ABOUT? Tony asked her.

William rattled his brain for a quick answer. THE DECLARATION OF INDEPENDENCE.

EWW! KIND OF BORING HUGH?

I LIKE IT. MAYBE ONE DAY THE LEARNING WILL COME IN HANDY WHEN I GO ON JEOPARDY AND WIN LOTS OF MONEY! LOL

LOL. Tony replied. I'LL CHECK WITH YOU LATER. PS I STILL WANNA C A PICTURE.

William closed his laptop and left the Underdog's office. He hopped into his truck and drove home.

In his home, he first kissed his wife hello, then went to their bedroom where he rummaged through the closet to find her old photo album.

"What are you doing Will?" his wife asked as she stepped in and observed him.

He extracted a small box from the highest shelf and turned to her. "I need a few of your old college photos," he spoke as he advanced to the edge of the bed and lifted the lid. He then pulled out the top photo binder and sifted through a few pages. He eyed his wife's beauty before taking hold of two pictures.

"I presume it's for one of your cases?"

He smiled at her and nodded.

"Don't make me out to be too trashy!" she joked.

Travis drove past the red barn and when he saw a large wooden sign indicating the title of the ranch, he turned onto the private drive. As he passed underneath the marquee, he and Saul observed a posted warning that read NO TRESPASSING.

"Let's be cautious boys," Saul told the team as Travis accelerated, but didn't speed too fast to stir up much dust.

The agents drove the half mile private drive around two bends and up a small hill before coming to a clearing. They spied the acreage, catching sight of the ranch house as well as a barn, a shed, a tractor and an off-road vehicle or two.

"I don't see anyone out and about," one spoke.

"Just the chickens!"

Travis parked and shut down the engine quickly. The bounty hunters grabbed their weapons as they exited the suv and hurried to their positions. Travis stood guard at one side of the house with a 12 gauge shotgun while Saul and Nathan went to the door.

After a second knock, the rancher appeared at his door. He told Saul that his nephew could be staying in an abandoned cabin up the creek a mile and a half and he last seen him a week ago.

"Does he carry a gun?"

"Yes sir," Mr. Scott replied, "You don't want to be without one in this neck of the woods."

The agents had the owner's permission to hike on his property through the back way. "We can't drive on the skid trail," Saul explained to the team, "If Darin sees us coming, he'd take off running and we might not catch him for days." He locked up the vehicle and with their tools of the trade at hand, they took off on foot. "Keep your eyes open boys, this guy is dangerous. He has assault charges and you heard his uncle, Darin loves to fight." They entered the thicket of pine trees toward the skid trail and started out on their treacherous journey.

William sat at the kitchen table with his laptop while his wife scrounged up some lunch for him. He used his cell phone to snap a couple shots of his wife's college photos, then he transferred them to his computer. He cropped the photos, copied, and pasted them to his facebook account.

In between bites of his sandwich, he typed in a message for Tony. HERE I AM. I TOOK A BREAK FROM MY REPORT TO POST MY PHOTOS. DONT BE MY FRIEND JUST CUZ IM PRETTY! LOL CHEYENNE. William waited for a reply.

U R CUTE, BUT YOUR HAIR IS OLD FASHION?
I LIKE MY LOOK!
ME TOO. Tony agreed. SO WHERE U LIVE?

BOISE. U? As he waited for an answer, he thought of how he could close in on the truth without dragging this so-called friendship on for days.

IM IN KELLOGG. I HAVE A QUESTION. U DONT HAVE NO FRIENDS? William tapped his finger onto his chin. I JUST CREATED THIS ACCOUNT THREE DAYS AGO. WHAT? U JUST COMING OUT OF OLD SCHOOL? HA! HA! I WAS SHELTERED. SORRY. Tony quickly sent back. IM JUST BEING A DICK. I NOTICED YOU LIKE TO GO TO CAR RACES? SO DO I. William typed in. ME AND MY FAM (MY DAD AND TWO BROTHERS) GO OUT TO THE RACETRACK ALL THE TIME. I LIKE THE STREET STOCKS BEST OF ALL. WE HAVE A FEW FEARLESS GUYS WHO ARE REGULARS AND ARE ALWAYS COMPETING WITH EACH OTHER. THAT'S HOW RACING GOES... William sensed his cocky attitude. YEA, BUT THESE TWO GO AT IT MORE OFTEN LIKE BEST FRIENDS GETTING REVENGE ON EACH OTHER. William pondered on his message, wondering if he was moving too fast. He thought of one of his own buddies who recently befriended a criminal in the same way he's working it over facebook and it took him two weeks to get his proof. William reviewed his statement, then sent it.

It didn't take Saul and his two man troop long to reach the skid trail. The sun beamed directly down on the clearing where they trekked while they spied for footprints or tire tracks of any sorts.

"It's getting hot," one complained as he stopped and took a drink from his water bottle.

"Let's step in the shade and take a rest," Saul suggested.

Nathan and Saul sat on a downed log and Travis on a small flat rock. He pulled a pack of cigarettes out of his pocket.

"You can't smoke!" Saul roared in a quiet manner. "It'll put off a smell."

Nathan watched his brother to see if he'd defy their large comrade who was put in charge.

"Darin won't smell it. He's still too far away." He stuck one in between his lips and cocked his eye at Saul who was now glaring at him, then withdrew the tobacco stick from his lips. "Damn it Saul. I'm dying here."

"You can smoke one as soon as we have Darin in handcuffs. Call it motivation."

The fugitive recovery agents returned to their venture and soon the skid trail became more narrow making it hard for the third person in line to see ahead.

Saul who was in the lead halted suddenly. He put his arm out with his hand up, signaling for them to be still. They stopped and listened. Everything seemed tranquil except for the breaking of twigs. Saul pointed towards the thicket which caused the two rookies to draw their firearms. When Saul stepped warily off the trail, Travis and Nathan knelt and watched him weave about in through the trees beyond and soon three birds came flying out. Saul turned and headed back. "It's only a deer," he whispered.

Travis and Nathan both sighed in relief. "My heart was pounding for a half a minute," one confessed.

A bit further into the journey brought an old dilapidated shed into their view. The men paused in their tracks while Saul used his binoculars to spy the area. "It looks clear, but you never know." He instructed Travis to stay to his left while Nathan was to close in on his right side, then the trio proceeded with caution.

Upon arriving at the structure, the bounty hunters observed the overgrown grass and shrubbery at the base of the door and alongside the exterior walls. They walked to the sides and noted the boards on the windows were still tightly nailed. "Nobody's been here for years. Let's keep going."

The team hiked over a ridge, then stopped briefly to spy the area before them. "Nothing yet boys." After he lowered his binoculars, they heard the cawing of a crow afar off.

"Something's over there." The rookies looked to Saul.

"Or someone?" He remarked as he raised his brows twice with pleasure.

The team headed toward the clamor. Every once in a while Saul paused and used his field glasses to try and locate the cabin. On his fourth attempt, he found it.

Travis borrowed the optical device and took a peek. "It's well hidden. I can see a portion of it," he stated, "but I see no sign of life anywhere." He handed the binoculars back to Saul.

"When we get a little closer," Saul told Travis and Nathan, "I want to approach the cabin the same way we did the shed; with our weapons drawn."

The time had crept into the second hour since William sent his last message to Tony and was waiting for a reply. In the meantime, he was catching up on paperwork and took a phone call from Devin, a bail bondsman from Sandpoint. There was a fugitive on the run that he needed The Underdog's to go capture. William glanced at his laptop and noticed he had a message, then clicked on it.

HEY CUTIE! I WASNT IGNORING U. MY BUDDY STOPPED BY WITH A JOINT. U NO HOW THAT GOES!

"Hmm.." William murmured to himself. "He's stoned."

SO.. WHAT WERE WE TALKING ABOUT? The message continued from Tony.

Cheyenne replied, I WAS JUST TELLING YOU ABOUT A COUPLE OF OUR RACECAR DRIVERS...

YEA I HAVENT BEEN OUT TO OUR RACE TRACK LATELY. TOO BUSY DOING OTHER STUFF. SO HOW MANY BOYFRIENDS U HAVE? LOL

"Darn it!" William sighed with discouragement when Tony changed the subject. He now knew it would take a few more days and a different play of words. HOW MANY GIRLFRIENDS U HAVE? LOL

The bounty hunters dodged trees and squeezed in between bushes as they neared the cabin, each staying alert to any sounds or movement. They had spread apart; one veered to the left and the other to the right while Saul went straight on. Saul was approximately fifty yards to the building when he heard a crunching of twigs beyond the brush. He glanced at Nathan who was some twenty yards away and gestured for him to follow. Saul aimed his 45 caliber and stepped slowly toward that way. At the next tree he caught sight of Darin who had made eye contact back at him.

The fugitive took off running in the direction of the cabin.

"Freeze Darin!" Saul yelled as he gave chase. "I'll shoot!" He exerted two strides, then hollered at Nathan. "Don't let him get in that cabin!" Saul tripped unexpectedly and fell onto his gut with his arms forward. His pistol went off.

Travis heard the gunshot and hastened their way.

Nathan had his firearm put away when he leaped over Saul and continued running in between the trees for their man.

Saul tried to stand, but instantly went down on his ass due to the pain that throbbed within his lower leg.

Darin was on the first step going up to the porch when both agents emerged from opposite sides of the house.

Travis ran faster than Nathan, reaching the mini staircase first. He leaped up the few steps and jumped onto Darin's back just as he opened the door to enter. He tackled him to the floor. "Quit resisting!" Travis roared as he sat atop of the fugitive's back and tried to grab his wrist. "You're toast Darin." He caught a glimpse of his rifle positioned upright from the floor just inches away. He began to pound with his closed fists onto the side of his face, noting his sword tattoos.

"Hit me again!" Darin thundered, "I'll file charges."

Nathan joined in on the struggle and soon their rough and wild fugitive was wearing handcuffs.

"Good job men," Saul remarked from the doorway of the cabin after limping to them.

Travis stood to his feet and lit his cigarette.

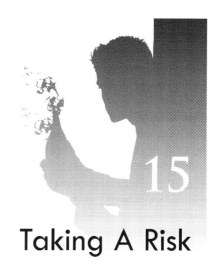

# Taking A Risk

I t had been three hours since Nathan and Travis brought down their last fugitive. After leaving the jail, Travis was dropped off at the Underdog's office and went home while Nathan drove Saul to the emergency room for an x-ray.

Travis parked in his spot and after checking his mailbox, he advanced to his apartment door. As he walked, he opened a letter from the county clerk and read it. He was being charged with Lewd Conduct with a Minor and was given a court date. "Great.. just what I need," he spoke with sarcasm, then entered his apartment and closed the door rather hard. He tossed his mail down onto the coffee table and relaxed onto his couch. He extracted his shoes, then raised and set his feet atop of his mail, atop of his coffee table. With his hands folded behind his head, he gave thought to his girl, wanting to see her, but not her mom nor talk to her mom. His cell phone rang. He lifted the device and saw that it was Hannah so he answered. "I was just thinking about you."

"I must of sensed it," she spoke with a giggle. "So are you still at work or are you done for the day?"

"I'm done. Just got home." He lit a cigarette. "What's up?"

"I have a baseball game tonight. It's the last one for the season. You want to come to it?"

"Yea. I have to shower and eat first, then I'll be over."

"Meet me at the ballpark, k?"

William telelphoned Nick and asked him if he was free from his roofing job to accompany him for the rest of the day to help catch a bounty. After he said he could do it, William left the Underdog's office and arrived at Nick's place to pick him up. Within the cab of the truck, William first showed his assistant their fugitive's mugshot. "His name is Kim."

"I know this dude! He's a roofer."

"When's the last time you seen him?"

"Oh.. a year or two."

"Well that don't do us any good now," William remarked, "I don't think."

"What did he do?" Nick took a second look at the printed out photo of Kim.

"Drug running, obstruction of a peace officer and he's a fugitive from justice. He only has a ten thousand dollar bond."

Nick knew it would be a quick paycheck for him, but didn't really like the thought of bringing in an old co-worker. "Where do we start?" he asked as he buckled himself in.

William sped off. "His listed address is in Coeur d' Alene."

Forty-five minutes later, they exited the freeway onto Sherman Avenue and detoured into the service station parking lot. After a quick break, William came out of the building wearing a bandana and his bullet proof vest.

Nick had his hair bound into a ponytail and he wore a vest in between two thin shirts. He also carried a taser while William kept his pistol in the holster on his side.

The two fugitive recovery agents returned to the road and headed to Kim's address.

"What does he drive?" Nick asked.

"I believe a teal thunderbird. It's in the file."

"That's odd. Usually a roofer would drive a truck."

"Yea?"

When the agents arrived at the house, two men and a woman were lazing about the front porch.

"None of them are Kim," Nick spoke after a glance.

"Until we get a closer look, we won't know for sure, but you're probably right." They exited the suv.

The group stared at William and Nick as they advanced up the sidewalk. "What do you want?" one called out rudely.

William and Nick continued to the edge of the stoop. "We want Kim!"

"He doesn't live here."

"According to our records, he does live here with his girlfriend."

The woman stepped forward and stood in the way of entry. "We broke up and he moved out."

"How long ago?"

"Two weeks."

"We'd still like to check the house and make sure he's not here."

"No!" she insisted, "That's my own private space."

"We understand that, but by law we can search the place because Kim named this address as his residence."

The gal looked to her friends for back-up. One of them stepped in close beside her with his burly arms crossed.

Nick placed his hand onto his hip just above his taser gun.

"Just let us take a peek," William urged, "then we'll be gone. I don't think either one of you would want to get the police involved.?" His face exhibited question while his tone expressed intimidation.

She exhaled as she glanced at her friend. "If I let you look for Kim, anything else you may or may not see in there doesn't matter?"

William agreed, then had Nick stand guard at the corner of the house while he went inside.

After a quick search, they left the property empty handed. While they walked the cement pathway, the ex-girlfriend recommended they go check out the Hogwash Bar down on Sherman Avenue. "He frequents there quite a bit."

William stopped. He turned and looked at her with a question. "Are you able to call and meet up with him?"

"Nope. You're on your own with that one."

He groaned within himself, then he and Nick returned to their Ford Explorer and sped away to the suggested establishment.

When the agents arrived at their destination, they couldn't tell if it was crowded or not inside the pub because of the connecting businesses and parallel parking. "I don't see his car anywhere."

The men entered the tavern and sat on separate stools. Nick lit up a cigarette and moved the ashtray closer in to him. When the bartender approached, William showed her Kim's photo.

"I've seen him in here, but not today." She paused. "He usually comes in with a guy, like a best friend and that's all I know."

William thought of what he could ask her, but nothing came to mind.

"You might want to try looking at Joback's. I hear it's a hip place to hang out. Just don't order anything there. I don't want to be a sellout."

The agents chuckled and said their thanks, then left Hogwash's and walked around the block to Joback's Pub & Grill. They entered the upscale eatery and repeated their actions of attending the bar stools and talking to the bartender. They received the same answer as they did in the previous drinking place.

When they were leaving, Nick stopped at the bulletin board because the word ROOFING had caught his eye. He reached out with his hand and took the advertisement prop. He read it aloud while William listened with much interest. "Kim's Roofing & Repair." Nick looked at his boss. "Could this be our guy? He started up his own business?"

William glanced at the business card. "This is great! We just need to come up with a plan." They continued to the outdoors and returned to their suv.

"There's no specific address on this card," Nick informed him, "Only Coeur d' Alene."

William took the card and looked it over. He took out his laptop and scrolled and tapped until an address appeared beside the phone number. "We have a place to go."

Within the minute, he had the address written down and was accelerating toward the location. Nick lit himself another cigarette and smoked on it during the duration of the drive. When they neared Tenth Street, they slowed their pace. Anticipation built as William braked. They spied the house and it seemed to have an absence to it without shades about the windows and no cars in the driveway. "It looks like no one lives here."

Nick jumped out and jogged across the yard to the living room window, then peeked in. He dashed back to the suv and reported his findings. "He moved. All the furniture is gone." He glanced at William. "That's an old card we grabbed."

"It might still be the same number though. We can call and see if it's still a working line, then call and ask him to meet us for a job."

"Where are we going to meet him?" Nick queried.

William kept silent with thought as he too wondered where.

Travis drove into the gravel lot near the baseball park, then parked his truck and exited on foot. As he walked toward the action, he observed that the game had started. He sat midway up on a wooden bleacher and cast his sights about, searching for Hannah. Her team was up to bat and she was standing at second base with her foot just off the plate, ready to run to third.

An hour and a half later, her team won the game. Hannah and Travis stayed at the celebration long enough to eat pizza and have awards. Hannah text her mom to let her know she was on her way home because she was to keep her younger brother company for the evening. She then cast her wanton eyes at Travis. "You want to come over?"

"I thought I wasn't suppose to come over?" He recalled the no contact order that the judge had enforced upon him, yet he knew he had already violated it. "If your mom or her cop buddies drive by and see my truck."

"She's dispatching tonight. Nobody but you, me, and Hans would know." She stepped in closer to Travis and kissed him.

"If I get caught or go to jail, we're done," he warned, "I'd have to break-up with you."

"You won't get caught. I'll make sure of that!" They kissed each other four or five more times as they stood beside her car, then they parted.

Travis followed Hannah to her home in Hayden and parked his truck around the block.

Hannah waited eagerly on the front porch for her man and after they entered into the house, she locked the door and drew the shades. She observed her brother to be sitting at the kitchen bar eating a snack and watching television. "Hey Stinky!" she called out. "We won our game."

"Hi Travis!" Hans ignored his sister and went straight for the testosterone. "Are you gonna stay and visit us?"

"Maybe."

"You can't tell mom," Hannah commanded to her brother.

Travis stepped to the eight year old who was smiling. "What are you eating?" He rolled his knuckles atop of his head.

"Are you trying to give me a noogy?"

"If I was going to give you a noogy, I'd do this." He wrapped his arm around Hans neck and he again used his other hand to roll his knuckles atop of his head.

He chuckled. "Ah.. Travis. You wait til you're not looking and I'll get you back."

"Promise?" Travis wore a grin.

William punched in Kim's Roofing & Repair telephone number on his cell phone, then pressed send. He turned on his speaker so Nick could hear.

"Hello?" A masculine voice came over the line.

"Am I speaking to Kim of Kim's Roofing & Repair?"

"You are," the man replied with a happy tone.

William nodded at Nick. "I took your card off a bulletin board and I've got a large roof I need re-shingled. Are you interested?"

"For the right price I am!"

"Come take a drive out here. See my roof and give me your bid." He gave their bounty an address after he agreed to meet him there in an hour. The agent expressed his urgency using a leaky roof.

William and Nick stopped in at Conoco for a break and to kill some time. To set his plan further in motion, William called his uncle who lives in Coeur d' Alene to let him know of the up and coming take-down at his house in an hour, then they drove to the relative's house where they waited in the company's Explorer from the side of the road.

Soon enough, a general contractor's truck pulled in and parked on the gravel in front of them.

"That's not Kim," Nick spoke as he watched the stranger exit his truck.

"No?" William cooed, then he and Nick jumped out of the suv and stepped to the man. "Kim?" William held out his hand with curiosity as he waited for his say.

"No, I'm Cecil." He shook William's hand. "Kim called and asked me to meet you here and look at a roof."

He eyed Cecil's small frame. "Where's Kim?" he demanded.

"That's irrelevant to this deal now," Cecil defended. "I more than qualified to give you a bid."

"The hell it ain't irrelevant." He raised the tone in his voice. "This isn't about a roofing job."

"Why are you getting angry with me?" The roofer challenged.

"We're bail Enforcement Agents and your boss Kim has a warrant out for his arrest. He was the one who was suppose to show up now."

"That isn't my problem."

"Maybe not. Where would Kim be at right now?"

"I don't know," the employee claimed.

"Oh you know." William's demeanor changed when he stepped toward Cecil and clutched onto his arm.

Nick saw his boss's move, then quickly grabbed Cecil's other arm and together the agents handcuffed him in the front and forced him into their suv.

"You can't do this to me!" The roofer now raised the tone in his voice.

"You're going to help us." William sent him a stern look as he hopped up onto the seat next to him. "How are you to get a hold of Kim after this meeting?"

"I was going to call him."

"That's a great answer," he remarked with sarcasm. "Cecil you need to persuade him to meet up with you right now."

While he sat in between the two bounty hunters still handcuffed, he dialed for Kim on his cell phone and put the device to his ear.

William and Nick glanced at each other, then watched Cecil as he talked. His phone's volume seemed to be set on high.

"The owner wrote a check for ten grand and I don't want to hold onto it so you need to come get it."

The agents heard Kim's sigh. "Okay. Meet me at the Fourth Street Conoco in ten," he told his employee.

Travis and his two players rested on the couch after a few rounds of hide n' seek. Hans kept bugging him to go one more time.

"I'll hide one more time, then I'm done."

"I'm staying here on the sofa chair," Hannah called out when Travis arose to go hide.

Hans closed his eyes and as he rested his forehead upon his crossed arms atop of the coffee table, he began to count.

Travis turned and went through the kitchen. He headed to the door that led to the garage and opened it. He moved through the passage in a stealthy manner and shut the door behind him. He cast his vision around the cubicle, wondering where to hide. The whole space was open except the corner where Kelly had parked her black Grand National. "That is definitely a sweet car!" he whispered to himself as he tiptoed to the fancy auto and scooted in between it and the wall, then dropped to his knees.

Within the minute, he went down to his stomach atop of the cement floor. He rolled to his back and scooted in just under the frame of Officer Kelly's Buick. As he lay hid from Hans, he eyed the sparkling black paint along the door and underside of the body. He moved his arm to his side and pulled his truck key from his jeans pocket, then brought it to his view. He lifted the pointy end up to the paint on the lowest part and began to etch. He scratched a one inch line, then another across the top of the first one, making a capital tee. He continued with an R, than an A until his name appeared with a silver glow. He thought it was awesome that the only person to see his markings would be the one who changed the tires.

Another minute and he heard the door from the kitchen open and he saw the light come on. He observed Han's shoes when he stepped in. While the young boy advanced around to the opposite side of the Grand National, Travis quietly went up onto his hand and knees and crawled about so he wouldn't be seen, but when he reached the front side, Hans caught him.

"Come on Travis," he bid. "Hannah wants you."

Travis pounced across the garage floor with Hans, then flipped off the light and closed the door. He returned through the kitchen and dining room to Hannah who was standing pretty.

William unlocked and took the handcuffs from Cecil's wrists, then sat on the passenger side in his truck. Cecil had agreed to drive him to the Fourth Street Conoco so it wouldn't seem suspicious to Kim. Nick followed them in the Explorer.

"Kim will be driving a red Chevy pickup," William sent a memo to Nick through voice command on his cell phone.

With only minutes to spare, they parked. Cecil and William in a space close to the street while Nick parked around on the far side of the pumps. The agent advanced from the suv and walked to the edge of the building. "I'm in position," he text back to

William quickly, then took notice that the gas station was a busy place so he figured he wouldn't stick out like a sore thumb.

"Copy that. Any second" he text back as he stood near the driver's door, yet out of Kim's view. He looked at his detainee who remained sitting in the cab, "When he drives in, I'll step around that van and get to his window before he can get out and ask you for that check."

"Okay," Cecil had to comply, "Then I'm going to drive away."

"Wait til he's parked to do that."

The agents waited three minutes more.

"That's him." Cecil pointed out as they watched him turn into the lot from the street.

William went his way to the rear of the van and waited. His adrenaline was flowing.

Nick stayed in position as he watched.

Kim drove in closer toward them and as he pulled into a parking spot two spaces down, he waved Cecil over.

With the fugitive's focus on Cecil, Nick carried his bean bag shot gun at his side as he hastened across the pavement toward the passenger's side of the red Chevy pickup.

William charged to the front of the van, then bypassed a car before creeping to the driver's side open window with his pistol drawn. "Turn off your engine," he ordered, "And let me see your hands."

As Kim sat idle with his hands atop of his head, he noticed from the corner of his eye, Nick at his outer window. He took a second look at his familiar face.

William lifted the door handle and forced the door open. He gestured for Kim to step out of his vehicle.

Nick came around the truck to assist in the handcuffing.

"Don't I know you?" Kim demanded of Nick.

William pressed Kim up against his truck and spoke close to his ear. "No you don't know him."

Nick reached into the red Chevy and took hold of the keys. He locked the doors and slipped the keys into Kim's front pocket before William escorted him over to their company vehicle.

"What happened Kim?" he asked of his court date.

"I was going to turn myself in after I took care of a certain matter."

"That's the typical line I hear all the time." He snapped Kim's seat belt into lock, then sat on the seat next to him. "And don't be mad at Cecil. We made him call you."

# Magic Moments

"**B**out time you get back!" Nathan shot a quick jest her way after she popped into the room.

"I've only been away for three days," Felica answered from a lying position as she floated in the air. "Why are you keeping track anyways?" Her eyes widened with curiosity. "Did you miss me?" As she waited for his answer, she focused in on his face; his large brown eyes and the half inch scar that lay across his cheek.

He looked upon he an saw a glow radiating from her countenance. "Of course I missed you Honey," he sported, "Where's my kiss?"

She flew his way, swooshing around his upper bodice, then stopping two feet in front of him. "Ha ha," she teased, then her countenance turned serious, "I can't.."

"That was hot!" Nathan blurted, ignoring her last statement. "Can you fly around me again?"

"No," she responded, then blushed. "And I can't be kissing any boys either."

"I don't see any boys here." He arose from sitting in his chair and was face to face with her. "Have you ever been kissed?"

"No, I've been locked up."

He could sense that she wanted a kiss and he wanted to know if kissing a genie would be like kissing a human. He reached out and placed one hand onto the back of her head.

Felica wondered why his hand was there when suddenly, he moved in. The force from his arm pressed against the crown of her head helped him to make contact to her lips. She was in a daze. When they broke, she opened her eyes. "You shouldn't of done that," she managed to get out.

He returned the look. "Why? Wasn't it good?" he joked.

"It was wonderful, but being a genie, a first kiss means you're betrothed to that person."

"Betrothed? Is that a whore thing?" He sat back onto his chair.

She chuckled. "No. Betrothed is a promise to marry. It's a part of our culture."

"Well," he hesitated, "I didn't know that and besides, it's not in my culture." He gave her an odd look and thought her engagement idea was illogical. "How are your parents doing?" he asked, wanting to change the subject.

The room was quiet. She sat up and positioned herself in an Indian style sit.

Nathan glanced upward and saw the beautiful genie staring at him. "What?" he innocently questioned. "You don't want to tell me about your mom and dad?"

"Don't you want to be betrothed to me?" she asked.

He smiled and glanced away when he heard her say that funny word. "It would be awesome, but I don't think I'm ready to get married."

"We can be pledged to one another for many years before marriage."

He cast his vision to his television set and thought on it while the commercial played. "But you can still have sex?" he challenged with a sly peek of the eye towards her.

"Silly!" she remarked, "Not til we're married. And you can't have sex with anybody else either."

"Just from a first kiss? No-way. You'd have to put out."

"Put out?" she asked with confusion upon her face.

He considered her virtuous ways. "Never mind," he said.

"Oh I'll find out what put out means!" she remarked as she snapped her fingers and disappeared into thin air.

William bit into a powdered doughnut after he lifted up the screen of his laptop and began the process of opening his facebook account. He was anxious to get scheming on a confession from Tony. The time was almost ten a.m. and he had slept in. While he sipped on a cup of coffee, he read his messages and pondered on his up-and-coming tall tale.

After some brainstorming, William's chat as Cheyenne started out with a simple HEY HOW YA DOING?

HEY GORGEOUS?? U DONT SOUND TOO ENTHUSED TODAY? Tony replied back to her.

I HAVE A LOT ON MY MIND. I SORT OF MADE A PROBLEM FOR MYSELF LAST NIGHT. William typed in, hoping to spike Tony's interest. BUT THATS NOT WHY IM CHATTING. I WANTED TO KNOW HOW YOU DID ON YOUR HISTORY TEST THIS MORNING?

OHH! U CARE?

OF COURSE I CARE. LOL William sent back.

I JUST GOT DONE TAKING IT THIRTY MINUTES AGO. I THINK I DID AVERAGE.

JUST AVERAGE?

MAYBE A B MINUS. NOW I WANT TO HEAR ABOUT YOUR PROBLEM. HAVE U BEEN A BAD DIRTY GIRL?

William moaned in disgust when he read his sexual message. NOT REALLY A BAD GIRL, he keyed in, I TOOK THE BLAME FOR A MINOR CAR WRECK. I LIED TO THE COPS AND MY MOM... He aimed for an early confession.

GO ON. Tony sent back.

"Darn it," he spoke to himself. IM FEELING REAL GUILTY FOR THE LIE IM IN, BUT I HAD TO PROTECT MY SISTER. THATS ALL.

IM AVAILABLE IF U NEED SOMEONE TO CONFIDE IN. Tony sent back.

William liked his reply, but still had to come up with more of a story. WE WERE IN A MINOR CAR WRECK AND I TOLD THE POLICE I WAS DRIVING THE VEHICLE. I WANTED TO PROTECT MY SISTER CUZ SHE HAS A SMALL CHILD AND SHE WOULD HAVE WENT TO JAIL FOR BEING BUZZED.

U GET HURT?

IM OK. MY ARM IS A LITTLE SORE. William fabricated for Cheyenne.

WHAT HAPPENED?

LETS JUST SAY WE RODE THE EDGE OF THE DITCH UNTIL WE CAME TO AN ABRUPT STOP. THE CAR WASNT 4x4 OR WE COULD HAVE TORE OUT OF THERE AND DROVE HOME ON THE BACK ROAD.

BUMMER! He remarked, then continued to type. I SUPPOSE AT SOME TIME OR ANOTHER IN OUR LIVES WE HAVE TO LIE.

"Bingo!" William said, then played on that. DONT TELL ME U BEEN A NAUGHTY BOY AND LIED ABOUT SOMETHING TOO? LOL

ME? NEVER. HAHA

OH COME ON.. I NEED U TO EASE MY GUILT.. William grew anxious to hear Tony's answer.

TELL ME ABOUT UR SISTER FIRST.

"Mmm.." he groaned, "Talk about a 180 degree turn." MY SISTER LOOKS LIKE ME, he composed instantly.

IS SHE UR TWIN

YEA. He said yes because he didn't have any other lady's pictures to show him.

IS SHE ON FACEBOOK

SHE DONT WANT A FACEBOOK ACCOUNT.

UR A WEIRD FAMILY LOL, Tony responded.

William paused. He didn't know what else to say to that so he leaned back in his chair with his fingers entwined behind his head and gazed at his laptop for a few minutes.

Tony worked on an assignment from a language arts class while he waited for Cheyenne's message. After some five minutes, he thought of their previous conversation, then typed in his confession. I LIED TO A COP BEFORE TOO CHEYENNE. IT JUST RECENTLY HAPPENED BUT WHAT CAN U DO HUH?

William jumped on the opportunity. WHAT HAPPENED? He used his own question against him.

LETS JUST SAY I GOT THIS GUY BEFORE HE GOT ME. THAT MOTHER F.. MADE ME MAD WHEN HE POINTED A RED LASER AT ME SO I TURNED IT AROUND ON HIM AND SAID HE THREATENED HARM TO ME WHEN HE CALLED ME.

BY LIEING? MY LIE WAS TO HELP SOMEONE. William stated in a clever manner.

WELL MY LIE HELPED SOMEONE TOO. ME! Tony reeked of pride.

U SOUND LIKE A SCALAWAG TO ME. A REAL VILLIAN! LOL

A SEXY VILLIAN? Tony jest.

William didn't want to reply. He hesitated telling any male he was sexy. He typed in a YES, then pressed the send key with his eyes closed.

Tony smiled when he read Cheyenne's yes. U THINK IM HOT HUH? DID I EASE UR GUILT

U DID.

SO WHEN ARE WE GOING TO MEET UP BEAUTIFUL?

CHRISTMAS? I HAVE TO GO. SOMEONES AT MY DOOR. William posted that last message to get rid of him. He saved and copied his evidence, then relaxed in his chair, glad to be done with that case. He glanced at his screen and observed a chat came in from Tony. He read it.

CHRISTMAS? Tony shot back. I CANT WAIT 3 MONTHS. LOL

William closed his laptop and when he looked up, his telephone rang. He reached across his desk and spoke his hello into the receiver.

"Hey William. It's Nick."

"Nick! Thanks for helping Saul catch Kim the other night."

"Sure." Time breathed in a quick pause. "I'm calling on behalf of my race car."

"What do you need?"

"Calipers and rotors."

"It'll come out of your paycheck," he threw at him.

"No way! You're one of my sponsors."

William wore a smile. "You get it painted and decked out with logo's yet?"

"Of course. I'm racing Saturday night," he told his number two supporter, then continued to answer his question. "I painted it brown and the numbers are yellow."

"Come on by and get some money."

"Thanks man and I have a snapshot of my race car. I'll picture text it to you."

Ian arrived home from school and sat with his mom at the kitchen table. They snacked on cheese sticks while they watched the two kittens play and run in the nearby area between the two rooms and hallway.

"What's my homework?" Dominique requested after she glanced at his Trapper Keeper that had been tossed down in a rough manner atop of the counter.

Ian had a good relationship and was close to his mother. He had been wanting to brag to her of his genie, but feared it she knew, he wouldn't be able to get the wishes he wanted so he sort of let her know of his genie in his own mind. "I have to write a story for writing class about What If I Had A Genie?"

"Hmm.. You mean what to wish for?"

"Sure. What would you wish for?"

"You know me. I would wish that everyone would get saved."

"A genie probably couldn't grant that, huh?"

"I'm thinking no because salvation is within the heart and it's a person's own choice to repent and accept Jesus Christ as their savior."

"Yap!"

"Other than that, I don't need a genie. I have everything I want. My sons, my writing, my house and pool," she claimed, "but most of all, my happiness in the Lord."

He thought for a moment. "You're gonna get me an F, huh?"

She stuck her bottom lip out in a joking manner, then moved her head indication no. "You write it then and I'll help you."

"Later Mom okay? It's not due til Monday." He stood to his feet and rushed off. He went up the staircase to his bedroom looking for his genie. He was hoping she had returned home. "Felica?" he called out softly. After no response, he changed into a pair of sports shorts with a matching sports shirt.

There came a small tap at his bedroom door with Nathan entering. "Hey bro. I've been waiting for you to get home."

"Why? Are you bored?"

"No.. I wanted to talk to you about you're last two wishes."

He listened.

"You have to set Felica free. She has betrothed me and wants to get married." He tried not to smile.

"What?" He expressed in a quizzical fashion.

"She has it in her head that because I kissed her."

"You kissed my genie?" he blurted out.

"Yes.." he quickly replied.

"Why?"

"I like her. I think she's hot."

"So now." he hesitated, "You're suppose to marry her? That don't make sense."

"Tell her that!"

There was a moment of silence.

"I don't know," Ian spoke of Nathan's request. "I already have my two wishes planned out."

"If you set her free she can leave and go be with her family permanently." He cast a grave look upon him. "That would be the right thing to do."

"You just don't want to get married!" he accused.

Nathan turned and left Ian's bedroom. "What a jerk," he remarked to himself.

Ian advanced to his door and with a push, it closed. He sat on the edge of his bed and thought of their conversation. If he set Felica free, he'd have to choose between being a famous rapper or having a stash of money.

Two hours had past since Ian wanted to see his genie when she finally appeared with a puff of green smoke in the corner of his room. He was experiencing timidness after he saw her, but spoke up anyways. "How was your visit?" he started with.

"It was pleasant and educational," she finished.

Ian remained at a rest in his tv chair watching wrestling. "Did you get to see all your family?"

"Basically yes. My mom and Pa, my grandparents and a younger sister I never knew I had."

"Cool. What's her name?"

"Cashelle. Weird name huh?"

He nodded.

Felica flew to the bed and sat upon the comforter so she could watch television with him.

Ian brought to mind, the bundle of money he anticipated to get. He thought his choice of cash would be the wiser and safer one for now, then he turned toward his genie. "I'm wanting my second wish."

She smiled. "Let me have it."

He felt his heart pound with excitement. "I'd like to wish for a million dollars of unmarked and untraceable bills to be put in a fireproof and waterproof safe."

"Wow. Did you memorize that?"

"A small safe," he quickly added, emphasizing the small.

Felica floated a foot or so in the air above his comforter. "As you wish," she told her keeper. She raised her left arm into the air in front of her and motioned a circle until a black cloud appeared near the ceiling and began to spin. The funnel slowly gyrated its way to the bureau.

Ian's eyes were wide and his mouth became gaped as he continued to watch the mini tornado turn back into a puff of black smoke. When the haze cleared, a black box rested upon his dresser. He grinned as he glanced at Felica, then again at the box. He jumped up and stepped to the fifteen by eighteen metal safe and touched it. "How do you do that?" he spoke under his breath.

"Open it!" she spoke in her angelic voice.

Ian reached for the skeleton key that was lying atop of the safe and inserted it into the lock. He turned the key and when he pulled on the handle to open it, he began to see stacks of green paper bills stuffed within the chamber. He laughed and sprang about, then stopped and took hold of one bundle. He thumbed the edges before lifting it to his nose for a smell. He returned the wad of money to its place and closed the metal safety box.

"Is that satisfactory?" Felica asked him.

"Oh yes. It is! Thank you." He turned and cast his attention to her as he spoke, then sat down in his tv chair. He returned his focus to his safe and pondered on where he would hide his loot.

"I have to go talk to Nathan," the genie remarked, "I'll see you later."

"Don't tell anyone about my cash, okay?" His brown eyes glimmered.

She zipped her lips shut with her thumb and index finger to show her silence.

Ian stepped to the dresser. He wrapped his arms around the small safe, tucking his hands underneath it and lifted. He then quickly set it back down. "Dang! This is gonna take me forever to bury." He locked his bedroom door and after some time, he managed to stash his metal safe in his closet onto the floor before anyone came to check on him. He knew it would sit for two or three days until he came up with a plan to entomb it.

# Race Day

Saturday afternoon came and Dominique gathered two of her sons for an evening of racing. This event was to be Nick's first time at racing and he wanted to get a feel of things for next year before this season ran out. She backed out of the driveway.

"Is Travis coming?" Ian asked his mom from the back seat.

"He said he might not make it because he has a dinner date with Hannah."

From the passenger seat, Nathan lit a cigarette and smoked on it while they cruised on Bunker Avenue toward the freeway.

Nick drove through the open gateway into the pit area, slowly by-passing the driver's concession stand, an American flag, and a set of bleachers. He noted the other cars and their décor as he made his way to an empty lane and parked. When he stepped out of his truck, he cast his eyes to the grandstand, observing the people that were beginning to arrive and claim their sitting spots.

Saul tailgated his co-worker into the pits and drove around the gravel loop before parking in front of Nick's truck. He stepped out of his vehicle and advanced to the rookie who was scanning the racetrack. "You ready to do this?" he asked.

"Hell ya!" Nick answered. "After I go check in and take care of the paperwork."

While Nick was off, Saul unhooked and removed the straps that held the race car to the trailer. He examined the fresh brown paint and the number 13 that had been outlined in yellow onto the spectators side of the car. He also noted and read a few of the sponsors' names such as The Underdog Bounty Hunters and a local auto supply retailer.

Nick returned. He went to his truck and grabbed his fire resistant racing coveralls. "One of those drivers was giving me the evil eye," he told Saul of the potential threat as he dressed himself.

"He's just trying to intimidate you. Don't take it personally."

"I wasn't."

The racer and his mechanical aide stepped to the rear of the trailer and took hold of the ramps. "Is your mom going to be here tonight?" The aide asked, then they set the ramp ends down onto the ground.

Nick glanced at his right-hand man. "Why yes she is." he used sarcasm with a grin. "And so is my girl Jen." He hopped up onto the trailer and climbed into his race car the way Bo or Luke Duke would have. He inserted the key and started it up. "Feel that power!" he boasted aloud as he revved the engine.

Saul looked on.

Nick shifted into reverse and as he looked in his rear view mirror, he carefully backed down to the ground, then buckled himself in and fixed his helmet onto his head.

Saul stepped to the car and bent down to the open window space. "It looks like you're ready to go. The engine sounds good." He stood and tapped the rooftop with a flat hand twice.

Nick accelerated toward the pit exit and stopped near the racetrack entrance at the signal of the official. As he waited for clearance, his gut churned with excitement. His dream was finally here; or at least one of them, he reasoned, then thought of Jen. He inhaled and exhaled a large breath, trying not to grin.

He held tightly with one hand onto the steering wheel and the other down on the ball of the gear shift.

The racetrack official waved him forward with a green flag. While he accelerated onto the oval track, he laughed. "Whew hew!" Nobody but God could hear him. He tested his steering by swerving to and fro as he cleared the first bend. When he rounded the second turn, he realized everyone in the grandstand was watching him. He became nervous, but immediately shrugged it off. He focused in on more speed for the straight-away. He braked for turn three, then pressed on the gas pedal as he came out of the fourth. He drove the straight-away and continued on for three more practice laps.

When Dominique, Nathan, and Ian arrived at the state line motor speedway, they searched the span of the pits from the highway and located Nick's car. They also observed that the drivers were beginning to run their time trials. Dominique slowed and turned left onto the gravel lane, then drove toward the free parking area and parked. They hurried to grab their snacks and jackets, then locked the doors to her explorer.

The roar of an engine speeding out on the track could be heard while they walked to the ticket booth to pay. The ticket goers entered and sat in their favorite section, five rows just north of the flagman. The three eager fans seated themselves atop of a blanket, then had to wait eight cars to see Nick run the two laps for his times.

Nick felt pleased with his times. When the time came for the drivers meeting, he went. He listened intently, yet he kept a smooth composure and when the pit official announced that he had made it into the four car trophy dash, he couldn't believe it. He wanted to burst. When the meeting was over, he headed back toward his car and Saul. As he walked away, he heard a rough voice erupt from behind him.

"Hey rookie?"

Nick turned and saw a much larger man than he, dressed in a racing outfit, standing twenty feet from him. Nick observed the mean expression upon his face so he cast his eyes about the vicinity, to his sides to make sure he was talking to him.

"What you runnin' under your hood?" the man asked.

"Three-fifty," he answered politely in spite of the driver's attitude.

"Don't let it go to your head!"

Two men dressed as mechanics appeared and stood beside the odd driver.

"Be careful out there. Bad things can happen." He turned and left with his pals.

Nick watched them retreat. "He just threatened me," he remarked to himself, then returned to his race car. When he saw Saul, he was too thrilled about racing in the trophy dash, he had pushed the incident about the menacing driver away.

Travis sat at a table with a drink as he waited for Hannah to arrive. He glanced at the time on his cell phone and read seven p.m. "The races are starting," he whispered to himself. He had wanted to go, only he had something else on his mind he needed to tend to.

Hannah stepped to Travis' table and seated herself. "Hi Baby." She observed the lit candle that was glowing from the center of the table. "Isn't this romantic." She leaned in to her beau and gave him a quick, but passionate kiss that said she missed him.

Travis noticed from the corner of his open eye, customers at the next table staring at them. He broke away from the moment with a little push. "Later Babe." They locked eyes. An invisible emanation from their love exploded about the dim lighting – they began to chuckle.

Hannah ordered a lemonade and relaxed into her seat a bit more while they studied the restaurant's menu between glances. Travis sent a kiss to her with a quiet smack of his lips.

She smiled. "So how is everything going for you today?"

He thought on that for a moment, then answered. "Everything is going great when I'm with you." He copied her smile, then returned to the menu.

"That's a good one Travis." She quit talking and looked up when the waitress approached and set her drink on the table with the promise to return momentarily. Hannah already knew what she was going to order for dinner so she just sipped on her lemonade through the straw while she watched the candle burn and flicker.

Travis set his menu down and snaked his arm forward to grab onto Hannah's wrist. "I want to talk to you about something."

She cast her eyes in his direction as she pulled her hand through Travis' grip until her hand met his. "I have something I wanna say too."

"You go first," he suggested.

"It's not a big deal," she spoke as her smile disappeared. "I was just going to tell you about my mother."

He raised a brow. "Anything about your mother is a big deal."

"She's being a rag again."

"Did she hit you?"

The waitress reappeared and quickly took their order. After she stepped away, Travis cast his eyes at Hannah and sent her a tacit expression, wanting an answer to his question.

"No, she didn't hit me," she replied softly. "Her attitude stinks. She's always watching me and nagging about every little thing. She even looked through my homework tonight."

"I'm sorry you have to go through that Babe."

"I just want to get away from her sometimes," she complained. "I'm ready to call my dad and see if I can stay with him."

"Where does he live?"

"Spokane."

"That's not too far away," he remarked, yet he had a different option in mind for her. "I went to court the other day."

"Oh!" she blurted out, "I was wondering how that went?"

"I plead not guilty which means my case will go to trial."

She leaned in close to him and talked in a low voice. "They want to prove you had sex with me?"

157

"Yes," he answered.

"That's disgusting!" She sat back in her chair with a frown and crossed her arms.

The waitress appeared at their table with appetizers; one plate held garlic bread and the other contained mozzarella cheese sticks.

The line-up for the hobby stock trophy dash was beginning to take place. Nick started the engine of his 79 Chevy Caprice and exited the pits. He drove out onto the track and stopped at the starting line where the four drivers were to be introduced.

Some five minutes later, Nick was driving in second position side by side with one of his toughest competitors. They both followed the pace car around the paved track.

Dominique sat on edge up in the grandstand as she watched her eldest son maintain an even start with the lead driver.

The pace car left the track. The cars' engines roared as they raced toward the green flag.

Nick pressed on the accelerator, bringing his car to full speed for the straight-away, then he took his foot off the gas at the start of the turn before increasing speed again for the next straight-away. He was determined to stay side by side with his rival until he could make his move.

Nick completed the first lap. On turn two, he had become entangled in a three wide with himself being the third car. He saw the front end of his machine going in too close to the cement wall. He couldn't turn left to avoid harm and the car hit. His right side threw metal sparks as it scraped the rock divider. The turbulence sent a rush to his gut, yet he didn't want to lose his position so he kept his speed up. He was able to press ahead of the middle driver who seemed to of backed off a car length. Nick steered inward, returning his car to second position.

"Yes!" Dominique and her two other sons cheered as well as many of the spectators.

For the next lap, he and the top racer fought side by side for the lead while the two other racers breathed upon their bumpers. The announcer was speaking his excitement into the speakers to the crowd. The white flag came out as they whizzed by the flagman for their final lap.

Nick was hoping his car would hold through the last two corners without sliding. His front bumper was just a foot behind the lead car's front bumper throughout the final turn. He didn't recoil when he accelerated at the close of the turn.

His family watched with wonder. "He could win it!" Nathan exclaimed.

The racers drove neck and neck toward the finish line. Nick held his steering wheel tight and pressed down on the gas as far as he could.

The crowd was roaring and the flagman waved the checkered flag.

"He wins it by a nose!" the announcer emitted, "Car number 13 Nick........Kerr.."

Nick couldn't believe it. "Yes!" he thundered and laughed within his car.

The crowd went wild, especially his mom and his girlfriend who arrived late.

Nick eased off the gas pedal, letting the engine return to an idle. As he rounded the turn, he observed Saul standing at the edge of the barrier waving his hat in the air and jumping. He could hear his pitman cheering as he passed by.

While the other three drivers drove to the pits, Nick kicked it around the racetrack to the finish line where the pace car and flagman awaited. His brown race car he named the Ole Bean Burner was parked facing the crowd. He took off his helmet, then quickly unlatched the seat belt. He climbed out through the window space with a big grin upon his face.

The trophy queen handed him his trophy. He gladly accepted the statue with a kiss from the hot brunette while he hoped Jen wouldn't get upset about the peck.

Ian stood at the fence with all the smaller kids in the grandstand who were begging Nick for his trophy.

"I'm keeping it," Nick shouted to his brother as he proudly held it up.

Travis popped the last bite of a cheese stick into his mouth while Hannah watched. He pushed the small plate towards the edge of the table.

"I don't want this case to go to trial," she protested, wanting to make her thoughts known.

"Me either, but if I plead guilty, they would have thrown me in jail for a long time." He paused while he took a sip of his soda pop. "My attorney said they will subpoena you."

Her eyes widened. "No!" She sat upright with a stiff back.

"Calm down Baby." He took hold of her hand. "I have a suggestion," he posed as his gut churned from nerves. "A wife can't be forced to testify against her husband."

Her face lit up and a smile appeared amid her blush face. "What are you saying?"

He too turned red in the face, but due to the dim lighting in the dining room, it didn't show. "If we got married, you wouldn't have to testify against me, then they'd drop the charge and we could live happily ever after." He anticipated a positive response.

She took a moment to think. "What about marrying for love?"

"We're in love," he answered with a sly, but honest tongue.

"My mom would never let me marry you."

"That's why we need to elope."

"I'm still underage. No one will perform the ceremony."

"Yes they will. I checked on-line. All we need is one parent to sign a consensual form."

Before Hannah could say anything, the waitress arrived with their main course. "Mmm.." she purred over her chicken fried steak and mashed potatoes with gravy, then glanced at Travis' plate. "Your dinner looks good too."

"Next time it will be tacos." He cut and forked a chunk of his steak. "You think your dad will sign that paper?"

"I think he will." She took her first bite. "So when do you want to elope?"

"Monday morning. Your mom will think you're going to school and Hans will be in school too." He continued to speak briefly of his plan, then he asked her if this is what she really wanted. If she really wanted to be married to the same man til death drew them apart, to share their money and have all the responsibilities of marriage.

"And all the sex I want?" she blurted as she raised her brows twice, trying to be cute.

Travis glanced at the people who occupied the table next to them, then he leaned in toward Hannah and whispered, "You're a nasty girl. I can't take you anywhere."

She replied yes.

Nick learned more about racing after experiencing some bullying in the heat race. Even though he finished in sixth place out of eight drivers, he still felt confident. He sat with the engine off in his car in fifth position at the pits exit waiting for the compacts to finish the last three laps of their race.

Saul stood at the barrier alongside the straight-away with the rest of the men from the pits who wanted to watch the bustle.

Finally the pit official signaled to the hobby stocks of their one minute warning. Nick started his engine, then he placed his right hand on the shifter and his other hand grasped the steering wheel. He was strapped in and ready to race, but this time he wasn't wearing a smile. Thoughts rang through his mind of that mischievous driver who stayed on his tail in the heat, trying to press and force his way through. He understood that was the name of the game, however, he speculated this number 10 was out to wreck him. He recalled Saul's words to not take the intimidation personally so he decided to make sure that bully didn't succeed at his plan.

The pitman waved the racers forward.

Nick cast a glare kiddy-corner at the number 10 car who was placed in fourth position, then he let his foot off the brake. With the gear set in first, he allowed his car to flow with the pack out onto the racetrack. His heart thumped and his foot was aching to go.

After one lap around the track, the green flag came out. Nick pressed the gas pedal down as far as he could speed without ramming into the car in front of him. The pack stayed tight throughout turns one and two, then on the straight-away, the car next to him on the outside fell behind while his foe advanced slightly ahead of third position. He accelerated and squeezed his way in between third and fourth positions forcing his foe to be against the wall.

When turn three came upon him, Nick's rival accelerated, clipping the front end of his car. Nick weaved which caused his car to slow and fall into the number six spot. "Whew.. That was a close one," he sported.

The race continued on for ten more laps without any problems. Finally, the two lead cars bumped and rubbed sides against each other until they lost control. One spun off into the dirt creating a cloud of dust while the other driver gyrated high. Both Nick and the other racers were able to pass around the scuffle through the dusty overcast. He could taste the dirt as he kept his speed.

Nick had three laps to go until the white flag came out. He was at the beginning of turn one when the bully in number 10 decided to hit his brakes abruptly which caused him to crash his front bumper into him. Nick's front end went sliding and his gut churned. He tried to keep his car straight, but this time, the hit was too much and it sent him into a spin. He braked to avoid hitting the wall or any other drivers. "That bastard got me!" he roared.

Nick regained control and accelerated back to racing speed. He glanced ahead at the flagman to see if he threw a black flag to number 10, but couldn't tell. The two new lead cars were already closing in on him, ready to overlap. On the last lap, he ended up passing the two slowest cars in the race, coming in in sixth place for the second time that evening.

When he entered the pits, Saul jumped up onto the trunk of his car, landing on his butt. He held on and hitched a ride back to the trailer.

Nick climbed out of his car and cast a glowing smile to his mechanic. "Not bad racing for my first time, huh?" he bragged.

# Slipping Out

Hannah parked her car at the high school where she attends in a space amid the other students' vehicles. She locked the doors, then as she walked toward the gate with her backpack, she tucked her cell phone and keys into her purse. She cast her eyes about to see if anyone was watching her. Finding it to be clear, she stepped off school grounds.

Travis sat in his truck with the engine running. He was ready to go. He glanced in his rear view mirror and saw Hannah walking his way. He scoped the road ahead looking for any police cars.

Hannah opened the passenger's side door and sat inside. "Hi Baby!" she greeted, then closed the door.

"I don't like picking you up at your school!" he let out, then looked in his side mirror. "It makes me nervous." He speed away knowing he could go to jail for a long time.

"Don't be nervous. If my mom drives by, she'll see my car and think I'm in school."

"I hope so." He paused to strike up a cigarette. "I don't need her to bug you at school, especially today."

"She usually doesn't and don't jinx us!"

He smiled as he accelerated to the next block and turned. He drove south on Ramsey Road to Interstate 90, then directed his truck toward Spokane.

Thirty minutes later and the young couple arrived in Spokane. Travis exited the freeway at the Maple Street exit and at the first crossroad, he turned right and headed downtown. He followed Hannah's directions down the one-way to a group of tall buildings. He located a parallel parking space in front of her dad's building and parked. After he shut down the engine, he looked out his open window at the city. "Your dad's a lawyer?"

"No. A financial adviser."

"Nice," he whispered to himself as he gazed upward.

Hannah took hold of her cell phone from her purse and looked at the time. "Almost nine. Are you ready to meet my dad?"

Travis aimed his face towards her and with an odd grin, he remarked in a high pitched voice, "Sure!" He paused, then spoke normal. "I don't know if you're dad will like me or if he will want to kill me, but I'm ready to meet him. What floor is he on?"

She chuckled. "He'll like you."

"He may not like my age."

Her chuckle turned to a smile and she carried a shine in her eyes. "I love you, so he will love you too."

"Stop it Hannah," he poked, "You're getting creepy now."

They stepped out of the truck and while they walked to the anterior door of the financial building, they held hands.

"Does your dad even know about me?"

"He does." Her answer seemed soft and brief.

"Probably all bad huh?"

"Not from me. Maybe from my mom."

"That don't make me feel better Hannah."

The twosome entered the business complex and rode the elevator up. Inside the enclosure all alone, they kissed and monkeyed a little until the door slid open to the seventh floor. Hannah led Travis down the corridor to her dad's suite. They stopped outside the door and cast their eyes at each other. She reached for the knob.

"Wait!" Travis blurted.

William sat at his desk and listened to his two voice messages, one being Travis calling off work for the day if anything did come in, the other was a solicitor. He then opened the file that Swade his bail bondsman had just dropped off and thumbed through the pages. "Timothy Mites," he read aloud, "Let's see what all Timothy did?" William moved his vision further into the folder until he came to the fugitive's list of offenses. "Hmm.. He's a burglar. Felony burglary, child endangerment and drug charges." He took a sip of his coffee.

The Underdog's office door came open with Saul entering in. He carried his own coffee mug as he advanced to and sat on the couch.

"Swade just left. We have a man to go hunt."

"That's why I'm here, to work." He sent an odd smile to his boss.

"Wise guy huh?" he cracked, then went silent on purpose. As he penned Timothy's number onto a piece of paper, he could feel Saul staring at him.

"Are you going to tell me about this case?" he spoke in a firm, deep voice.

William glanced at the agent to see if he was frowning, then he looked again, but this time he gave a tantalizing smile. He closed up the folder and held it out for Saul to come and grab.

"Toss it to me prick!"

William chuckled, sensing Saul's humor.

Saul lifted the file cover and browsed the information while William took hold of the telephone receiver and dialed the contact number that he had jotted down.

A man answered the call with a relaxed hello.

"Timothy?" William began.

"Maybe. Who is this?" he shot back.

"How the heck are you? You missed court."

"Is this the bail bonds office?"

"No it's not Tim. I'm the bounty hunter who's going to bring you in."

"No need to hunt me down," he replied, "I'll come in."

"Why'd you miss court?"

"It slipped my mind."

William expected more of a fight. He arranged to meet up with the fugitive in one hour, then ended the call. He cast his attention to Saul and remarked, "That seemed too easy."

The two agents hastened to put on their gear, then left the office. Saul drove, advancing to Bunker Avenue to pickup Nathan before jumping on the freeway to the city.

Travis' decision was to wait in the corridor while Hannah went into her dad's suite to confront and ask him for his blessing and a signature. He leaned with his forearms onto the window sill and looked out the huge tinted windows at the traffic below. He was heavy in thought. He figured if he couldn't marry Hannah today, he would even be in more trouble for taking her out of state. He reflected on her being alone in that office appealing to her father. Feeling like a coward, he realized he needed to be by her side so he stood vertical, turned himself, and walked to the door. He twisted the knob and entered into the first of many rooms. He scanned the newly decorated lobby and noted another closed door. He looked to his side and saw the receptionist sitting behind the check-in counter. He took his cell phone out of his pocket and began to text Hannah.

"Can I help you?" the office employee asked him.

"Not really," he replied, "I'm with Hannah." He cast his attention back to his cellular device.

Within the minute, Hannah opened a door and gestured for Travis to come with her. "I just asked him," she whispered while they stepped through the hall back to her dad's office.

"What did he say?"

He didn't have time to answer.

Hannah's father stood to his feet when they entered, then put out his hand for a shake. "So you're the young man who has stolen my daughter's heart?"

Travis smiled, then replied. "Yes sir." He stuck out his hand midway to meet his future father-in-law for that handshake.

"Go ahead and sit." He eyed Travis' stature and his style of clothing; his half inch combed hair that had been laced with gel and the thin silver rod he had pierced through his eyebrow. "You don't look like a bounty hunter to me?" he poked, "Where's your large muscles and bad ass tattoos?" He flexed his own biceps.

Travis laughed. "I'm still working on the muscle part. I work out two or three time a week." He felt somewhat at ease.

"I use to work out." He returned to sitting in the chair behind his desk. "I'd have you call me John, but I hear you would rather call me dad?"

Travis grinned. "Yes sir," he piped again as he cast his eyes to Hannah who was smiling back at him.

John leaned forward on his desk and crossed his arms. "So you are telling me that you love my daughter?"

Travis sensed the start of the interrogation. He looked at John and replied, "I do love your daughter. I'll treat her right and.." he paused as he glanced at Hannah, "I hope we live happily ever after."

John chuckled lightly. "Nobody lives happily ever after.." He turned his focus in on Hannah. "You said you weren't pregnant again so why can't you two lovebirds wait at least a year to get married?"

"It's something we need to do right now just for us," she spoke, trying to persuade her father.

"Is it a legal matter?"

Neither answered.

"Well, you seem happy. Does your mom know?"

Her eyes strayed aside while she answered with a soft no, then she peered at her dad. "That's why I'm here."

"I don't want your mother calling me up wanting to talk." He used bunny ears to emphasize the word talk.

"I'll handle mom when the time comes." Hannah retrieved the legal paper from her purse and handed it to her father.

Fifteen minutes later, the happy engaged couple left the large business complex and returned to their truck. Travis sped away. He applied his driving skills to whiz through the traffic safely as he headed for Interstate 90. Upon the ramp, he and Hannah heard the specific beeping from her cell phone alerting her of an incoming text.

"It's my mom," she said with wonder, then read the text aloud, "I had to come to your school – oh shit!" She glanced at Travis. "Two students were fighting.. and she wants to know where I am exactly."

Hannah pressed the reply key. "I'm in class," she typed in and sent it.

Travis puffed on a cigarette as he drove east through Spokane.

A minute passed with another text. Hannah read it, then cast her vision onto her beau. "Now she wants me to meet her on my next break."

"You can't," Travis stated with authority, "We're on our way to get married."

"I know Babe." She texted her mother back saying she couldn't meet her.

Officer Kelly was disappointed that her only daughter couldn't sneak in a minute, yet she didn't want to interrupt her daughter's education so she put her cell phone away and jumped into her patrol car. Her fellow worker had already left with one in custody. Kelly started to accelerate through the school's parking lot when she saw a student she recognized. She let down her window and braked. She called out to the young gal. "Cassie – Is that you?"

Cassie turned and waved. "Hi Hannah's mom."

"You haven't been over to our house in a while?"

"I've been busy. I really have to get back to class. Tell Hannah I hope she gets to feeling better."

"Why?" she hesitated.

"Isn't she at home sick today?"

Kelly was disturbed by what she was hearing, yet she played along. "Yea.. I'll tell her."

The teenager turned away.

Officer Kelly rolled up her window and stepped on the gas to make her exit. She drove two blocks and parked with her radar turned on. She retrieved her cell phone from her pocket and instructed it to dial her house telephone. When the answering machine came on, she ended the connection, then pressed the keys to make contact directly to Hannah's cell phone.

Hannah was heavy in thought about the marriage ceremony as she gazed out the passenger's window at the highway signs that whizzed by her view; the building, the fields and the incoming mountains. Her dreaming suddenly became broken when her cell phone rang. She observed it to be her mom, then turned her head to question Travis. "Why is she calling me? I'm suppose to be in class." Hannah didn't answer the call.

"Who knows what she's up to?" Travis remarked.

Some thirty seconds later and it rang again. She wavered on answering it, finally pressing talk.

Kelly spoke with a firm tongue. "I know you're not in school. Are you sick?"

It wasn't a normal thing for Hannah to lie to her mother, however, she expelled the best word that came to mind. "Yes."

"What's wrong?"

"Just girl troubles," Hannah replied.

"Where are you at now?"

"I'm driving home."

"I just left your school. Why didn't you tell me that when I text you?"

The young gal didn't say anything.

"Hannah?"

"Just leave me alone Mom," she vented, "You're treating me like a child. I'll be okay." Her hand quivered as she ended the call.

Travis stayed quiet and listened as he continued driving. They crossed over the border, returning into Idaho.

Officer Kelly had a gut feeling while she drove back to the high school, then hastened through the parking lot, finally stopping at the bumper of Hannah's car. She glared at the parked automobile. "That girl is up to something," she groaned to herself, "And I bet she's with that Travis!" Kelly accelerated out onto Ramsey Road and set her sights for the police station.

The three Underdog agents arrived in Coeur d' Alene ahead of scheduled time. They exited the freeway and turned left onto Sherman Avenue. Saul drove some eight blocks before turning into the parking lot of the only grocery store on that street. Saul advanced to the far side of the building where he backed the suv against the cement wall and parked. Each agent watched in a different direction for their bounty.

"This grocery store isn't very busy," Nathan commented as he scanned the area, "I count ten cars and two trucks."

"That's why this is a great place to meet someone." William opened Timothy's file and scuffled through some papers. "According to this info, he drives a dark blue Toyota truck – an older model," he added.

Ten thirty came and went with no sign of their fugitive. Feeling frustrated, William took hold of his cell phone and pressed Timothy's number, then waited for him to answer.

Timothy was sitting at a red light in his blue Toyota pickup when he answered the call.

"I don't like to be stood up!" William growled at him. "Where are you?"

"I need more time." His reply was heard aloud over the speaker.

"How much more time?"

"Tomorrow."

"Oh hell no! You need to meet us now to get this warrant taken care of."

"I have a few things to do first. I'll call you back." He closed the slider on his cell phone.

William glanced at Saul with a scowl. "I'm calling him back." He looked down at his cell phone and aimed his finger toward the send button.

"Hold on! I heard a familiar sound in the background," Nathan blurted as he thought about it. "A boat whistle."

"I heard it too," Saul spoke with eagerness, "Let's head over to the lake."

Saul turned the key to start the engine, then shifted into drive. He flew out of the parking lot and sped toward the city center.

Timothy accelerated his blue Toyota pickup out from Third Street onto the main artery that led to the downtown area. He headed away from the meeting spot, yet he didn't go far; he had to stop at a red light. As he waited for the traffic light to turn green, he cast many peeks in all three of his rear view mirrors. He knew he had driven too close to the grocery store before he had second thoughts and changed his mind.

Saul raced through two yellow lights before catching up to the slow traffic.

William rolled down the passenger's side window and stuck his head out. With a breeze in his face, he used the binoculars to scan the traffic ahead. "I think I see him," he spoke as he returned to the inside of the cab. "He just turned onto Sherman."

The excitement of a car chase filled the air while Nathan sat attentive, ready for some action.

"Come on." Saul drummed his thumbs onto the steering wheel while he waited for the slow traffic to get moving under the green light. He finally accelerated and crossed over the intersection, then changed lanes and gained the lead until he was slowed again by another vehicle.

William popped his head out the window for a second time and saw their fugitive making his way onto Northwest Blvd.

Making it through the next light, Saul maneuvered the explorer back to the original lane that he started from. He sped ten mph over the speed limit as he drove alongside an over-sized truck to avoid a cop. He pressed on the gas pedal a bit more to try and catch up to Timothy. "Keep your eye on him!" he exerted to William and his binoculars.

Timothy exited from Northwest Blvd. He took the ramp up to Highway 95 and while he waited for a clear shot to turn right, he observed in his mirror, a black suv rushing up to his bumper, then stop suddenly. He cast his eyes at the driver and saw an unfamiliar face glaring at him so he gunned it. The tires spewed a spray of sand and pebbles.

The agents were surprised at Timothy's getaway, then bolted after him.

Timothy hastened and turned onto Lincoln Way. He sped past some apartment buildings, then failed to slow down enough for the next street. He overshot the curb and sideswiped a street sign.

"Awesome!" Nathan cheered as they sped through the turn. "He totally bent that sign down!"

Saul followed the fugitive as he advanced east onto Harrison Avenue. He observed his blue truck weaving from side to side hoping he didn't smash into another vehicle.

Timothy honked his horn as he approached a slow car. "Get out of my way!" he roared within the cab of his truck.

The snail paced auto didn't budge.

Timothy pressed on the accelerator and swerved out into the oncoming lane. He raced past the sluggish auto and darted back to his original lane. He sped ahead to escape the agents' immediate sight.

"That boy has to be on drugs!" one remarked.

"Or just desperate."

Saul glanced in his rear view mirror, then with a heavy foot, he also hastened to get around the slow moving auto. He barely made the pass when the oncoming traffic arrived and honked. "Whew!" Saul exhaled.

"Holy cow Saul! Who's the one on drugs?" the rookie agent blurted as he grabbed onto the overhead handle.

Saul and William kept their eyes on the road ahead.

Timothy led the agents through three green lights, then turned left onto a side street and drove two blocks. He went left and advanced one block, then turned left again, then again at the next corner, making a complete circle.

"What the hell?" The bounty hunters were puzzled at his way.

Timothy made another left turn.

"I have an idea. Let me out up here." William unbuckled his seat belt and when his co-worker slowed at the next corner, he jumped out of the vehicle. Saul kept following the blue truck as it continued on its circular path.

Timothy looked in his mirrors after each turn. "What a bunch of losers!" he chuckled to himself of the chase. "They really think they're gonna catch me?"

The next block came. William waited for their bounty to draw near, then he darted out from behind a parked truck and rushed to the driver's door. He leaped and clenched his right hand onto the roll bar. "Stop your truck!" he thundered as he continued to reach through the open window of the cab with his other arm and grab onto Timothy's long ponytail and pull. "Stop this truck I said! You have a warrant."

"I don't care!" Timothy shot back as he struggled to push William off the side of his truck. He cranked the steering wheel causing his truck to veer up a driveway and cross a yard, tearing up flowers and destroying a gnome.

"Oh wow!" Saul snickered when he saw William's ass hanging from the open window with his legs running alongside the blue truck.

William threw his fist, making contact to Timothy's upper cheekbone while he continued to persuade him to brake.

The truck dropped from the curb onto the street as Timothy's foot came off the gas pedal.

Saul sped to catch up so he could help in the stopping of their fugitive. "Get ready Nathan!" he shouted, then drove to the front of Timothy's truck and swerved into it, hitting the bumper. The blue truck veered into a vacant lot.

Amongst the verbal chaos and struggling, Timothy pressed the brake.

William ripped open the door and pulled him out.

Nathan leaped from the rear seat and joined in. He helped William slap a pair of handcuffs on their fugitive before he stepped to his truck and shut the engine off. They shoved their bounty in the back seat of their suv without buckling him in, then they jumped in while Saul stimulated the tires to get away from the area before the cops arrived.

# Letting Go

Officer Kelly parked her patrol car at the station and after she checked in with her boss, she changed into civilian clothes and left in her own car. She first drove through the parking lot of the high school to catch another peek at Hannah's car before heading to her house in Hayden. While she drove, she wondered what her daughter was up to. Was she getting ready to runaway or worse, elope? Kelly had to hurry.

Travis and Hannah returned to Coeur d' Alene from their excursion to Spokane, exiting onto Northwest Blvd. They advanced to the downtown area and parked close to the Federal Building where they met up with Dominique.

"This is kind of sudden?" Dominique commented to her son as she approached them, "but I'm glad you called me so I can be a part of your special day." She stepped forward and gave Travis a hug, then turned to Hannah. "I'm so happy to meet you." She exerted a softer hug onto her soon to be daughter-in-law.

Travis disclosed to his mother a brief explanation of his doings and the doings of the state while they stood about his truck. "We have to get married..."

Hannah reached into the cab of Travis' truck and grabbed her backpack. She felt herself begin to shake from being nervous.

It was really going to happen. She thought and feared how her own mother would react to her young marriage.

Travis dropped his cigarette to the ground and mashed it with his shoe. "I suppose it's about time we head inside." The trio walked toward the court house.

Officer Kelly parked in the driveway and made haste to exit her car and go into her house. Once inside, she tossed her purse and keys onto the kitchen's peninsula and scurried to Hannah's bedroom. She stopped in the doorway and stood with her hands on her hips while she cast her eyes about, wondering where to start searching.

She stepped to Hannah's desk and scanned the worktop, noting that her ipad wasn't there. She then moved her eyes to the nightstand and noticed the electronic device wasn't there either. Kelly pulled open the top drawer of the desk and shuffled about the knickknacks, then skimmed through a stack of papers until her eye caught sight of a small box. She lifted the small jewelry box and with much anticipation of seeing a ring, she opened it.

Kelly stepped to Hannah's closet and skimmed its contents. She believed only a few articles of her daughter's clothing were missing. Afterwards, she snooped through her dresser drawers, then ended her search at the nightstand. She withdrew a receipt, seeing that the logo belonged to an elite department store. She read the description and cost, realizing it was an elegant shirt and two accessories. "Why would she need these?" she asked herself as she observed the date of purchase to be yesterday.

Kelly dropped the receipt into the drawer and closed it. She walked out of the bedroom and returned to the peninsula where she retrieved her cell phone. She pressed send to redial Hannah's number and let it ring until the voicemail came on.

Inside the Federal Building within the restroom, Hannah was donning herself up special to be a bride while Travis and his mother waited in the main corridor. Travis wore a dress shirt and tie and his hair was gelled and combed back.

"Is she saved?" Dominique asked him.

"She said she is a Christian," he answered with confidence.

She was silent as she hoped in her heart of Hannah's salvation, then reminded her son briefly of what the Bible says about marriage.

"It'll be okay Mom." He turned away as though he didn't want to talk about it. He knew he loved her and had to marry her or go to jail.

Moments later, Hannah stepped into their presence.

"Oh wow!" Travis remarked when he saw she wore a lacy white blouse and a matching ribbon within her updo hair style. "You look so beautiful." He advanced toward her.

She blushed.

"No kissing the bride yet!" Dominique jested.

"Your mom's right Travis."

The bride and groom went into the clerk's office to check in before entering into the courtroom to face the judge.

Because of her daughter's defiance, Kelly left the house and returned to her car. She drove to two nearby churches where she and her family once attended. The first church building was vacant of any cars or members so she sped to the second place of worship. The parking lot consisted of some twenty vehicles, yet she didn't see Travis' truck.

Curiosity led her to park her machine and go sneak a peek. She came upon the door and opened it just enough to know a marriage ceremony was taking place. Her heart fluttered as she squinted to see details of the bride.

The usher stepped in her view, startling her. "May I help you?" he asked.

"Oh.. no," she reacted suddenly, "I was just searching for my daughter Hannah."

"There is no one here by that name ma'am," he whispered.

"Sorry to bug you." Kelly turned and as she hustled back to her car, she realized a wedding of that sorts was too costly and needed much preparation. "Why would anyone get married on a Monday anyways?" she asked herself. She peeled out of the church's parking lot and set her sights for downtown Coeur d' Alene.

Travis was finally able to kiss his bride after they were pronounced husband and wife. The couple then walked out of the Federal Building with their marriage certificate in hand.

"Congratulations! May God bless your marriage," Dominique expressed her happiness for them. "And thank you for including me." She eyed her daughter-in-law's ring.

"You want to go eat lunch with us Mom?" Travis asked.

"Yea, that would be great."

"We're heading to The Rib."

"Okay, I'll meet you there in about ten or fifteen minutes?" She observed his nod, then turned and walked to her vehicle.

Kelly made her way to the Marriage Post in downtown Coeur d' Alene. She parked her car alongside the curb and stepped out. She placed an arm atop of the door and stood within the open space where she looked up and down the block to see if she could spot out Travis' truck, then spied the small parking lot across the side street behind her as well as the area in the rear of the chapel.

With no sign of her daughter, she stepped back, closed the door and advanced around her car. She walked across the lawn toward the building, entered in with caution and saw the place to be empty of people except for a man who approached and asked her what she wanted.

Kelly presumed he was the minister. "I'm an off-duty police officer and I'm looking for a young woman who may have been married here today?"

The chaplain thought before he answered. "I married two. Do you have a picture of her?"

She retrieved one from her cell phone collection and showed him.

"No. Neither were her."

"Alright. Thank you." She turned to leave.

"Did you try the courthouse?"

She glanced back at him. "That's my next stop!"

The newlyweds advanced to their truck where Travis opened the passenger's door to let his wife sit down, then he hurried around to his side. He tucked the special document behind his seat, then jumped in. He inserted the key into the ignition then was startled by a woman banging on Hannah's window. "What the hell?" he blurted.

"It's my mom!" Hannah spoke in a panic.

Her door came open. Kelly reached in and took hold of her daughter's arm. "You're coming with me!"

"No I'm not!" She tilted herself backwards until her shoulder touched Travis. She pressed her leg against the door frame to keep herself inside the cab while her mother continued to grab and pull. "Stop it Mom! You're hurting me."

"Quit resisting then," she shot back.

Travis threw his door open and jumped out. He ran around the hood of his truck and leaped in behind Kelly. He grabbed onto her belt with one hand and wrapped his other arm around her waist to try and remove her from Hannah's lap. "Leave my wife alone!" he thundered as he applied his bounty hunting skills to extract her.

Kelly let go of her daughter and after Travis released her, she stood upright. "Your wife?" Her green eyes throbbed as she glared at him.

Travis felt the presence of trouble. "Yea, my wife. And I can prove it!" he blurted.

Her hands were on her hips. "Let's see your proof of this marriage?" Her tone sounded like a woman ready to rip the judge's endorsement to shreds.

Hannah remained sitting in her seat as she listened.

Travis wore a growl upon his face and after reconsidering his words, he answered with a no.

Kelly exhaled heavily. "I don't honor your so-called marriage... Hannah, let's go."

"Why not?" Travis demanded.

She then pushed Travis so he slammed up against the side of his truck. She turned and reached into the cab again for Hannah.

Hannah was stunned at her mother's outrage. "Leave me alone – I'm staying with Travis." She was now standing in the door space between her mother and her husband.

"You're only seventeen years old!" Kelly scolded as she buckled one of her hand's onto Hannah's pants at the waist. "That means you're a minor. I can have a lot of cops here real fast."

"You rag!" Travis called her. His face was bathed in displeasure.

"Travis?" Hannah stepped to him, but was stopped by her mother. "I'll just go home with her for now, I don't want you going to jail," she spoke out, "We'll have to work something out later."

He was silent as he leaned his back end against his truck wanting to call Kelly's bluff, but didn't feel like dealing with the police either. He cast his eyes to Hannah. "Grab your purse." His heart ached as it ripped with sadness and anger.

Hannah had some tears drip from her eyes as she complied with them both.

Travis lit a cigarette and walked around to the driver's side door of his truck. He stood alone as he watched his distraught wife sit into her mom's car and ride off. He thought and wondered what he could do about this situation. Maybe he would consult with William on this or maybe even an attorney.

Ian arrived home from school at his usual time of three o five. He encountered his mom and brother in the kitchen talking about their busy day. One talked of the fugitive he and his fellow workers just chased in the suv within the south side of Coeur d' Alene while the other buzzed of her short lunch with Travis. "He's not a happy groom right now," Dominique spoke as she cuddled and petted her favorite kitten she calls Kitten Little.

"Travis got married today?" Ian sought confirmation on what he just heard. "Who'd he marry?"

"Hannah."

"I don't know her."

"None of us did." Dominique set the small animal down on the floor. There was silence amid the air while they watched the two young cats play. Cobra hiked up her back to make herself look bigger as she pounced toward her sister. "We need to have her over for dinner or a barbecue as soon as things cool down, huh?" she suggested.

"Yea, that sounds good," Nathan agreed, then took off to his bedroom.

Ian followed. "Are you going to play video games?"

"After my shower."

Ian entered his bedroom anxious to see his genie. He saw that she was sitting in his game chair frantically pressing the buttons on his x-box controller so he sat on the edge of his bed to watch.

"Hey." She observed him from the corner of her eye as she continued to focus in on her near win.

Ian soon arose and stepped to his closet. He moved the sliding door some ten inches and stuck his head through the gap to take a peek at his safe. He gasped when he saw it was gone.

"Your mom took it," Felica stated when she heard his short intake of air.

He turned to her with a puzzled look. "Why was she in my closet?"

"She was hanging your clean laundry on those hangers."

"Dang it," he groaned under his breath, then closed the shutter in disgust. He stepped to his bed and sat with his back against the wall. He pulled his legs up to his chest and bowed his head into his lap. He sat still for a time as he pondered and thought, then lifted his head and looked at his genie who was now floating comfortably in the air. "I'll just use my last wish to wish for another million dollars."

"Sorry," she replied, "but you can't repeat a wish."

"What?" Stunned by her answer, he returned to thinking.

A minute passed when he and his genie heard footsteps in the hallway nearing the bedroom door so while Felica made herself invisible, he turned his eyes to see who it was. "Mom?" His call was stern.

Dominique knocked and entered. She stopped within the doorway and looked upon Ian with a foreseeable expression as she waited for him to speak.

"Why did you take my safe?"

"Where did you get it would be the question?" She returned with her own inquest.

"I found it."

"Really? Where?"

He was silent as he cast his eyes down at the carpet.

"What's in it?"

"It's just an empty safe. Can I have it back?"

"Open it and show me it's empty."

"I lost the key."

"Sure.." she hesitated. "Find the key then we'll see if you get it back." She turned and left the room.

His anger arose. "I hate you!" he yelled as he stood to his feet then advanced to the open door and slammed it shut.

Felica stayed out of sight as she watched the spat.

His bedroom door flew open. "Don't you be slamming doors in this house!" she ruled with a firm tongue

Ian didn't say a word, but rather turned away and waited for her to leave. His brow was crinkled and every muscle in his face had grown tight. He moved toward the window and waited for her to re-close the door.

A soft voice came whispering throughout the room. "Are you okay?"

He had grew weary of always being watched even in the privacy of his own bedroom. He took in a deep breath and exhaled, then replied with rudeness to his genie, "I want to be left alone now! Can you leave?"

"And go where?" She appeared from her invisible state.

"Home to your family."

She carried a puzzled look upon her face.

Ian cast a glare at her. "I just want all this to be over," he blurted. "My last wish is to set you free because I need my privacy back." He stepped to his game chair and after he sat, he began to think and reflect on what he had just said.

There was a tap at the door with Nathan entering in. He sensed the tension as he stood eyeing the disturbance.

Felica had started to cry, then withdrew to her unseen state.

Nathan looked at his brother. "What's going on?"

"She's free to go."

"You set her free?"

"Yea." He looked away.

"Wait Felica!" he bellowed as he turned and focused in on the vicinity where he last saw her. "Come talk to me in my room." He darted out of Ian's bedroom, then when he entered his own bedroom two doors down, all was silent. "Felica?" he called out, then stepped to his large wicker chair and sat. "I just want to say good-bye before you go."

Felica had followed Nathan to his bedroom, but couldn't talk. She thought it was because she had been weeping, but then she felt herself evaporating from his existence. She managed to produce a small poof of green smoke within the air for him to see before she vanished.

Nathan arose and as he stepped forward, he reached his hand up into the near faded mist and was awed. "Felica?" he whispered, "I do love you..."

The time had been an hour since Dominique scolded Ian for slamming his bedroom door. She trekked upstairs to see if he had found the key to that safe. She knocked lightly and pushed open the door. "Ian?" she sought while she cast her eyes about his empty bedroom. Her vision stopped at his window when she noticed that the screen had been cut. She inhaled abruptly, then advanced with speed toward the metal framing and examined it further. She poked her head through the severed wire and looked down at the ground to try and figure out how he descended from the second story. "Why didn't he just go out the front door?" she wondered aloud, then began to worry.

Dominique pulled the glass pane closed and locked it. She stepped to his dresser and quickly opened a few drawers. She noted that his clothes were still in there place so she left his room.

She called his two friends, then searched around the neighborhood for two hours. She began to wonder if she should call the law.

Nathan who was looking parched in the face, entered the house through the kitchen door and grabbed himself a pop from the refrigerator. He plopped himself in a chair at the kitchen table near his mother. "Nothing," he reported.

"You're a bounty hunter and you can't find him?" She was sarcastic, but punning with her remark.

He gave her a crooked smile, then wondered if Felica had anything to do with his brother's disappearance. "I'm gonna go check his room."

"I'll go with you." She set her Mountain Dew on the table and headed for the upstairs of the house.

Nathan peeked into Ian's bedroom, then decided to go on to his own room.

Dominique spied underneath Ian's bed and in his closet, then as she stood idle in the center of his room, she heard a moan coming from the corner behind the entertainment center. She stepped forward to the edge of the wooden structure and peered through a gap. She beheld her son who was slumped in the corner with his eyes closed. "Ian?" she spoke softly.

Ian opened his slumberous eyes to see half his mother's face through the crack. "Mom. I fell asleep," he replied before he remembered his missing safe, then he sat up.

"How'd you get back there?"

"I'll show you." He used his hand to push onto a section of the thin wood on the back of the entertainment center, then he crawled through the opening. With his head appearing from the bottom shelf, he climbed over a pile of video games to the carpet.

Dominique reflected on his secret little passageway as she watched him, realizing it was the second item in his bedroom he had butchered. "I've been looking for you for two hours." Her tone turned from concern to being annoyed. "Why'd you cut your screen?"

"I was mad. I wanted you to think I ran away."

"Well you did a good job at it." She paused while he yawned. "Did you find the key?"

"I had the key." He sat at the edge of his bed. "Mom – I need to tell you something."

Dominique perked up as she gently sat onto the nearby chair, keeping her attention in on her son.

"I got that safe from a wish."

She wrinkled her brow. "Huh?"

"This might be hard for you to believe, but I found a genie in a bottle and she gave me three wishes."

She chuckled. "I don't know what to say to that."

"Remember the mirror from the attic? You believed that."

"Wow." She was amazed as she listened further into Ian's tale, finally becoming convinced when they opened the safe and she saw the cash. She reached in and grabbed a bundle, then looked it over, even smelling it. "You can't keep this money."

His heart sank when he heard his mom say that. "Why not?" he asked.

"Because this money came from somewhere. The government or FBI would eventually trace it back to you and they would not believe your story of a genie!"

After some thought and disappointment, he agreed. "Can't I keep just one bundle?"

"Why? What would you buy?"

"A go-cart."

"Why didn't you just wish for one?"

He bowed his head. "I should have, but Felica was still a secret."

She groaned. "We have to burn this cash." She then turned to him with a suggestion. "Maybe I could buy you one next spring when you turn 14."

"Really?" His face lit up.

"But first you have to buy me a new screen with your allowance." Dominique shoved the wad of money back into its place and closed the safe.

"Mom – I'm sorry. I don't hate you." He wrapped his arm onto her shoulders.

"Even if I wasn't buying you a go-cart?"

"Yes. I was just mad," he indicated once again of his temper.

"Well don't keep anymore secrets from me. It causes trouble."

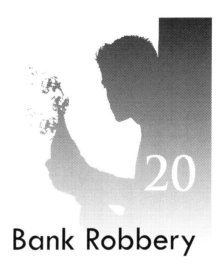

# Bank Robbery

Travis fussed to his mom and brother of Hannah's disappearance. The day was now Friday and he had become more concerned because he hadn't seen nor heard from his wife all week. "I've given her and her mom four days to work it out," he stated.

"Have you tried to call her?" Nathan asked.

"I called and text her, but I think her number has been changed or disconnected and her facebook has no activity on it either."

"Hmm," Dominique hummed with wonder. "What are you going to do?"

"I want to drive over there, but knowing my luck, I'll get pulled over by a cop or Hannah's mom will call the cops."

"For what? Inquiring about your wife?" she jawed.

He thought of the restraining order.

"It sounds like Officer Kelly is just a big bully!"

"She is," Travis replied in agreement.

There was a pause.

"I'll go with you," Nathan offered.

"Let's go."

The two brothers left the house with their mother looking on. They seated themselves into Travis' truck and sped off.

With cigarettes in between their fingers and the windows rolled down, they drove on Bunker Avenue to the freeway, then Travis accelerated west toward the city.

William and Saul sat at their desks in The Underdog's office listening to the police scanner as they waited for Swade to arrive with the information on their next bounty.

The scanner beeped causing the two agents to turn their heads and look. While talk came through the speakers, the strength meter showed its red lights.

"The call is close by."

They kept their attention to the action.

"A 2-11?" one questioned in awe as he glanced at the other agent.

"Armed robbery," the other defined.

The bounty hunters listened to the officers who were reporting to dispatch of their findings at The First State Bank as they gave details of the robber to be a male of about five feet seven, weighing some two hundred plus pounds and he was wearing all black, including his mask.

"He's a short guy."

They continued to give ear and soon learned the perpetrator was still at large.

"We should take a quick run uptown."

The office door opened and Swade entered in with a file in his hand. He stepped to William and set the paperwork on the desk in full view, then sat in the chair opposite of him.

"Who do we have to go catch this time?" William bid with a smile, then pulled the file close to him for a quick study.

"His name is Bobert Curry."

"Bobert? What kind of name is that?"

Swade shrugged his shoulders. "He supposedly lives in Mullan and he's disabled. He's not really a bad fella, but he missed court and his phone's been disconnected so bring him in and I'll re-bond him."

William agreed with a nod. "We'll get right to it," he said as his brain registered the scanner beeping with a brief 10-4 from one of the officer's.

"I need him by Monday morning," the bondsman concluded as he stood to leave. He reached forward and shook William's hand. "Send me a text after you nab him."

The office door came open once again, this time it was Nick who entered in. "Hey guys, I saw your vehicles parked outside and thought I'd drop in to see what's up?"

"Perfect timing," William stated, "We just got a bounty. Wanna go?"

"Yea. I could use a few extra bucks." His eyes caught sight of the scanner when he heard some static. "I saw two cops racing toward the other side of town." he said as he remembered the fast going patrol cars.

"Someone robbed the bank," William told him.

Nick seemed amazed. "I wonder who?"

Saul returned from the backroom with a bulletproof vest for Nick. "Someone who is short and chubby," he answered the rookie.

William grabbed the file, then stepped to the scanner and flipped the switch to off before leaving the office. The trio climbed into the company's suv and drove away.

Saul was curious about the robbery and knew William and Nick were too so he headed the back way toward the crime scene. The bank was attached to a row of businesses that aligned McKinley Avenue, one of the main roads uptown. Saul advanced onto Hill Street and drove to Railroad Avenue where he passed by the ball field, then accelerated south up a one-way lane until he came upon the hind part of the buildings.

The agents noticed the alley was blocked by police barriers in the direction of the bank so Saul turned into a parking lot and parked.

"Let's get out and see what we can learn," William suggested.

Travis exited the freeway into the city of Coeur d' Alene and drove north to the town of Hayden. He became anxious as he neared the street where Hannah lived with her unpredictable mother so he lit a cigarette and smoked on it to help calm his nerves. He turned onto Miles Avenue and drove some three blocks before turning onto a side street, then he accelerated at a normal speed past her house.

"The drapes are pulled shut," Nathan reported, "And I don't see anyone."

Travis made a u-turn at the next street crossing and parked down the street on the opposite side of Kelly's house. He didn't see Kelly's car, but he knew she could park it in the garage. He continued to puff on his tobacco stick as he spied the neighborhood to see if anyone was watching him. "I have an idea," he spoke to Nathan with a glance. "I'm gonna get out and walk in the alley."

"Are you serious?"

"I think so," he answered with confidence, however, he stayed idle.

Nathan griped his hand onto the doorknob and looked at Travis. "Don't be a chicken. We're bounty hunters."

"I know, but Kelly's so intimidating."

The two brothers were soon crossing the street and walked the sidewalk past the corner lot until they came upon the alley. They directed themselves onto the gravel lane and advanced to the fourth property. Travis stepped to the tall wooden gate and after scanning the windows of the house, he entered the yard.

"I'll wait here," Nathan called out in a whisper as he watched his brother.

Travis stopped in his tracks to turn and look at him. "Chicken!" he mouthed, then continued on toward the house. He crept up to Hannah's bedroom window and peeked in through the small gap between the blind and sill. He didn't see any sign of his wife so he took in a deep breath and tapped on the window.

The Underdog team didn't get far in their quest. They were only a block away from the bank when they were stopped by two policemen.

"What are you men up to?" one officer asked as he and his partner noticed they were wearing bulletproof vests and black attire.

"We're investigators," Saul remarked.

"Were you called to this job?"

"Yes sir."

"Let's see some identification."

The bounty hunters remained quiet for the moment while they showed their ID's. The sound of static with some talk could be heard coming from the law enforcers radios.

William waited for the cop to look at him. "You have any leads yet?" he requested with boldness.

"All we know is that he disappeared out the back door and no one saw what direction he went nor what kind of car he drove away in – Some think he fled on foot."

"The bank has a back door?" Saul questioned, thinking that was odd.

"Downstairs where the bathrooms are. I'll show you." The lead officer returned their driver licenses, then expressed his desire to escort them to the crime scene.

The agents glanced at each other with skepticism. Saul then gestured with an extended arm and a flat hand to point the way for William and Nick to go.

William peeked at his cell phone, noting the time to be almost 5:30. He followed the group into the alley behind the old brick structures and stopped at the first wooden door. He looked at the city cops. "Has anyone searched inside these buildings?"

"I believe so, but the thief wouldn't be in there. He'd be long gone by now."

William thought the officer seemed naive in his thinking and continued on. He and his team checked the locked doors and peeked into the windows that weren't boarded up while they walked to help their investigation seem real. He knew only four places in that row of buildings were vacant.

A call came over the officer's radios in which one responded, "We're on our way." He turned to the agents. "Good luck in your search. We have an unruly person to go arrest."

William and his team watched the uniformed men hustle toward the street to their patrol car.

"This one is unlocked," Nick spoke low as he pulled the door open with a creak, then the three of them slipped inside the abandoned business without being noticed. Nick closed the door. William cast his attention to Saul. "That was a close one!" he scolded him of his fib. "They could have hauled us off to jail."

"But they didn't." he shot back with a grin, then lit a cigarette. He and the agents ambled around the dark and dusty expanse eyeing the old wood floor for anything unusual. They also observed boards that were stacked alongside the decrepit walls with empty shelves, some looking as though they were ready to fall to the floor.

"This reminds me of the YMCA building next door," William remarked. He took a few steps, then turned about suddenly and beheld Saul.

"What's that funny look for?" he asked.

"The bank robber is James Lolly! The description of the suspect fits him to a T."

Nick stepped into the conversation. "You could be right."

"Heavy in thought, William paced the floor. "But how did he slip away so easy?" He tried to explore a way within his mind.

"He just walked home," Saul put forth his thought.

"You mean ran home?"

"I bet that SOB is already sitting at home counting the money, Nick commented.

William froze in his tracks. "He used the underground tunnels to get home! That's why no one saw him."

Saul stepped to where his boss stood. "There has to be a trap door close by then, right? At least that what comes to my mind from what you've told me about these tunnels."

"Yes, I agree." He gestured for his men to separate and go search more thoroughly in the different areas of the large building.

Travis' face barely reached the bottom of the closed window. He tapped on Hannah's bedroom window a second time, then quickly moved his eyes to each side of the house to see if anyone was approaching.

Hannah popped her head into view and smiled when she saw her husband. She also noticed Nathan standing afar off at the gate.

"Open the window," Travis called out in a whisper as he motioned with a hand for her to slide it.

"I can't." Her words were muffled through the glass. "An alarm will sound if I do."

"That's crazy! Your mom has you trapped inside?"

Her countenance changed. "My mom wants me to get an annulment."

"Do you want one?"

She shook her head no.

He put his mouth close in to the crack between the two panes. "Neither do I. Go out the front door and come out here." He heard a whistle and turned toward the direction of his brother, but instead, he saw Officer Kelly creeping alongside the house with a pistol aimed straight at him. "Oh shit! Don't shoot!" he called out as he stumbled backwards.

"You get out of here!" she commanded.

Hannah witnessed her mom's demeanor and began to scream. "Mom! No." She spun herself around and grabbed hold of her desk chair, then threw it at the window. It broke the glass with a loud crash and two of the chair's legs came poking through. The alarm sounded within the house.

"You're on my property!" Kelly thundered with a glare in her eyes.

"Mom – stop it!" Hannah continued to yell throughout the ordeal. "Put that gun down!"

"No!"

Travis' heart was pounding. "Your daughter just broke her window out and you're worried about me being on your property?"

Officer Kelly flashed a peek at Hannah and saw her to be standing at the window. "She's okay. She's not bleeding."

"How do you know?" He glanced at the window. "Hannah, you okay?" he shouted for her, but she had left their view.

Nathan's mouth was gaped as he watched and wondered from the edge of the fence if he should grab a large rock and hurl it at the crazy woman.

Travis started to retreat using sidesteps through the back yard when he saw Hannah rush around the corner of the house with a cell phone to her ear. "I called 9-1-1!" she hollered to them.

Kelly lowered the pistol and headed towards her daughter. "Give me my cell phone!" she demanded as she tried to rip it from her grasp.

Travis ceased from his backward motion when he beheld Kelly's attack on his wife. With the pistol now off of him, he rushed toward the commotion.

"Why are we looking for James Lolly anyways?" one asked William. "We need to go get Bobert."

"We have all weekend to catch Bobert." His tone was firm as he spoke. "James is Swade's bond too and we need to protect Swade's investment so I want to catch him first. He thinks he has the cops fooled," he bragged, "but he doesn't have me fooled!" He used the toe of his shoe to examine the corners of the floors, then he pressed his fingers onto the folds on the walls. "I'm not seeing any trap doors."

"Nothing over here either," Saul reported of the far corner as he turned and headed toward the door.

Nick was empty handed as well.

"Let's get out of here – quietly, and we'll go see if James is at home."

The two smokers mashed the cherries of their cigarettes and deposited the butts into their jeans pockets.

Saul pushed open the old creaky door and peeked through the gap. He didn't see any law enforcement in the alley or out yonder in the parking lot. "Coast is clear," he sent back to William and Nick who then followed him out of the building. They walked together through the narrow passageway back to their suv.

William grabbed his binoculars and a small 12 inch shovel. Nick gave him an odd look.

"It's to help us dig." He thought more on the idea. "You still want to tag along for the evening?"

Saul overheard his question. "What's your plan?" he asked as he stepped in closer to them.

"Don't know yet, but I'll be prepared if we have to go into the tunnels." He also grabbed a flashlight and shoved it in his back pocket.

The two bounty hunters and their sidekick took off walking in the opposite direction of the bank. They came upon the back end of the abandoned YMCA building and kept going west, by-passing one more building. They turned left and advanced alongside that building until they reached a cement stair unit. They climbed the seven steps, then crossed McKinley Avenue and trekked up a steep side street. When they came to the top, they crossed the one lane road in which James and Linda Lolly live on.

The agents hiked up a small grassy hillside to a flat section of an old dirt road and stood near some trees. William spied James' property as they all panted for air. "I'm not seeing any movement over there," he said to his team.

"Me either," Saul added as he peered with a naked eye. "The front windows sure have some large shades drawn over them."

"Yea," William agreed, then scanned the area above and behind them to see if anybody from the condominiums or the street above was watching him and his agents. He returned his focus in on the bank robber's home with the binoculars to his eyes, observing James' black truck to be parked on the grass, then he viewed the close up of his apartment once again. "There's no way of telling if he's home unless he comes outside."

"I have an idea," Nick proposed, "I'll go knock on his door and ask if he has any rooms for rent."

"I don't think you have to now." Saul reported as he noticed a man approach James' apartment door and knock. Saul waited to see if the door came open and after he watched the tenant walk away empty handed, he turned to Nick. "I have something else I want you to do for me."

Officer Kelly had her pistol aimed down at the ground while she used her empty hand to grab her cell phone from Hannah's grip. "Give it to me!"

"My mom is acting crazy." Hannah managed to spill out to the 9-1-1 dispatcher before the device was ripped from her ear. Her mother's fingernail caught on her face. "Ouw!" she cried out as she wore a scowl upon her face. "You scratched me!"

Travis slinked in behind Kelly and clutched onto her wrist. He used all his strength to keep the pistol pointed downward while he tried with his leg to trip her.

Nathan ran across the yard to help his brother disarm and take her down.

Hannah watched in horror as the two most special people in her life struggled. She yelled for her mom to stop as she touched her sore cheek.

Officer Kelly brought her left fist around and smacked Travis alongside his head giving him a temporary daze.

Nathan lowered his hard body and prepared himself to tackle the stout woman. When he made contact and the three of them dropped to the ground, the pistol fired.

"Aahhh.." Hannah screamed as she fell onto the grass ten feet away, then grabbed her leg.

"Hannah?" Kelly hollered while she was being held to the ground by the two bounty hunters.

Nathan kicked the gun from her control and it lay on the lawn.

The anger Travis carried in his heart for this barbaric woman was great. He wanted to let loose and throw a couple of punches her way for all the trouble she had caused him, especially for the abortion, but he chose to not hit her. He figured his mother raised him better than that. He turned his attention to his injured wife and stood up. Nathan backed away as well.

"I abhor you!!" Hannah screamed at her mother in the midst of her agony, not aware that the police had arrived.

Two officers rounded the corner of the house. "Everyone freeze!" both hollered out as they aimed their pistols forward.

Kelly's heart sank because she realized what he daughter had just said was true. She saw it in her eyes. "I only tried to do what was best for you," she told her.

"I don't care anymore."

"What happened here?" the first officer asked in a firm manner while the other one radioed for an ambulance.

"My mom shot me!" Hannah yelled to them. "That's what happened."

The officer who asked the question recognized Officer Kelly Stone. He knew her as an outspoken and honorable law enforcer. He stepped to her weapon and picked it up with a pencil, then proceeded to slip it in a bag for a possible fingerprint analysis.

"These two men are trespassers!" Kelly charged as she stood to her feet.

"She was going to shoot me!" Travis retorted to the deputies, "Just because I was talking to my wife who she had locked up inside her house."

"No because you were on my property." Kelly shot back to try and change the subject.

"Everybody be quiet!" The cops commanded.

They heard the siren of the ambulance come roaring up the street. The paramedic parked the diesel and shut down the noise.

The law enforcers talked to the off duty officer first, then Hannah, and finally the two brothers together. No charges were brought to anyone at that time and there would be a report filed. One officer told Travis he didn't see any protection order concerning him pop up on his screen and it was also stated to Kelly that she couldn't keep her seventeen year old daughter locked up like a prisoner. Hannah's a married woman and free to go.

Travis stood next to Hannah and the gurney she lay on. "I'm gonna ride with my wife to the hospital," he told the medical technician, then cast his sights to Nathan and asked him to follow in his truck. After he nodded, Travis tossed him the keys while they loaded Hannah in.

With tears building in her eyes, Kelly stepped away and disappeared into her house. She would have to collect her pistol from the captain when she returned to work on her next shift.

The bounty hunters sat onto two large rocks underneath the shade of a tall pine tree awaiting for Nick to return with a crowbar. The temperature read 78 degrees and was cooling down fast as the sun began to set behind the mountains. William and Saul kept their eye on James' apartment and at one point, a patrol car approached slowly up the one-way lane toward them, but they didn't worry because they concealed themselves behind some bushes.

Nick transported the Underdog's suv from the parking lot behind the YMCA building to the street above the hillside in which the Reo Hotel was located. He parked and locked the doors, then descended a wooden staircase that had been built on the side of the hill. He walked to the pine tree where William and Saul were laying low. He knelt and handed the metal tool to William.

William caressed the bar as he stood to his feet. "Are you men ready to do this?"

The thrill seekers took off walking down the dirt trail toward the hotel with William in the lead. He carried the crowbar at his side as he came upon a small patch of grass fitted with a dumpster, then the one lane road. On the left side of the pavement sat the little oval house which contained two apartments, the farthest one being James'.

William glanced into the covered porch to see if anyone was outside smoking a cigarette. "The coast is clear." He urged his team forward as he crossed the road and headed for the basement door.

Music was heard coming from the facade apartment. He looked that way and saw that the shades were drawn. Saul grabbed and lifted a chair that blocked the basement entry, then moved it while William put the crowbar to the door hinge.

A slender, but aggressive man stepped out from the hotel door and advanced their way. As he lit a cigarette, he saw the crowbar. "What are you guys doing?"

"We're plumbers," Saul threw at him.

The man observed their black clothing and the shovel that William had sticking out from his back pocket. "No you're not." He turned to leave.

Saul panicked and grabbed onto the man's arm. "Don't be so anxious to leave!" He bullied the stranger by pushing him to the open door. "Get down there!"

The man seemed stunned at Saul's command and dropped his cigarette to the cement.

William stuck his face into Saul's view. "What are you doing?" he asked, but went along with the course of action when Saul forced the man to step down the staircase. Nick hastened down the steps behind Saul while William closed the frayed wooden door.

Down in the basement, Saul threatened the stranger with a shove to the wall. "Don't you make any noises or you'll get a fist to the mouth!" He then observed an old dusty chair in the corner of the small room and snatched it.

In the meantime, William and Nick descended a second set of steps and entered into the old boiler room.

"Follow them," Saul instructed the man, then carried the chair with him. Inside the dim enclosure, Saul handcuffed the man's hands behind him to the one seater.

While the bound up man sat, he watched the bounty hunters as they opened another door, then climb some horizontal boards and crawl onto a pile of rocks until the first agent disappeared. "Take me with you!" the curious stranger called out to Saul before he reached the top. "I won't tell anyone."

Saul turned his head toward him. "Just stay put. If you see James Lolly, you can whistle for us." He continued on to join his comrades.

In the tunnel, Nick pulled out two pocket-sized flashlights and handed one to Saul.

"Thanks dude. You'll make a good bounty hunter some day," he jest.

William led the way as they walked into the eerie darkness. "You think James could be in the swimming pool again?" Nick quizzed his boss.

"I don't know," William answered, "but what I do know is that we need to be quiet. I don't want him to hear us coming." The agents followed the narrow passageway until they came to an intersecting tunnel. They turned east and headed in the direction of the bank.

The tunnel seemed rugged. As the bounty hunters crept along over the rocks and dirt mounds, dust sprayed from the top when heavier vehicles passed above. They trekked on through for nearly ten minutes, finally stopping at two connecting tunnels to investigate.

"This one goes up to the McConnet Hotel, I bet ya," William whispered, then turned and continued to press forward toward the bank. Within twenty feet or so, the tunnel ended with a pile of slabs blocking their way. The agents shined their flashlights upward and observed a crawl space. "I'm going in boys," William informed them, "I believe this could be the entrance."

"Be careful boss," Saul cautioned as he watched Nick drop to his hands and knees so William could use his back to lift himself up. "You don't want to run into any cops when and if you reach a trap door."

William managed to squeeze himself into the space with inches to spare. He shined his flashlight upward and saw sewer lines and the foundation of the building. He smiled big then moved the beam of light forward and noticed the space to be wider. He was able to crawl the few feet to a gap that ran horizontal then stood on his knees to radiate his light for a better view and saw a wooden panel. He began to hear footsteps and voices and knew he found the way James had escaped.

While he studied the panel with his finger, he recalled the police officers revealing to him and his men of the alarm sounding from the back door of the bank and no one saw the robber after that. William figured the trap door opened up to the bathroom or a closet, but wasn't going to pursue it any further. He knelt on all fours again and maneuvered his way back to Saul and Nick. "This is definitely the way he came," he spoke in a whisper as he rubbed the dirt off his hands. "We now need to find the money so we can prove it was James."

"That might be easier said than done." Saul commented, "And hiding the money underground would be a very clever idea."

"We think so, but the authorities have no clue about the tunnels yet, so it's up to us to try and find James' loot," William expressed further determination. "Let's check every crevice and gap as we head back."

The bounty hunters searched for odd markings or traces as they backtracked through the tunnels. When they came upon the passage that went to the YMCA building, they stopped and shined their lights above the blockade. "You want to?" William asked of the two if they were up to climbing and going in.

"No," Saul replied after inspecting and seeing no sign of foot traffic. "Something tells me he's gonna hide the money closer to home."

The agents continued on toward the Reo Hotel. "At least we know the way he escaped, huh? We can tell the detectives that much even if we don't find the money or James," Nick offered.

"Hold your tongue young man," William sported.

The tunnel rats neared the opening to the old boiler room with William to be the first to scale the pile of slab. When he crawled over the top, he heard clatter and saw James breaking their prisoner free from the chair. He quietly reversed himself, then scooted to the edge and dropped to the ground on his feet. "James Lolly?" he voiced with authority.

James seemed startled to see William. He glanced at his tenant and ordered him to leave. "No police!" he yelled.

The man scampered up the staircase before William had a chance to lunge and grab hold of him.

"What the hell are you doing in my basement again? I have no warrants." James roared at the bounty hunter as he took notice of Saul surfacing from the tunnel.

"Where's the money?" With a stern look upon his face, William scanned his suspect for a weapon.

"I don't know what you're talking about. You and your pal." He saw Nick descending from atop of the slabs. "You and your pals need to get out of here. You're trespassing!"

William detected the stink of alcohol. "Maybe so," he replied, "but we just found the way you came after robbing The First State Bank."

Saul sidestepped two feet alongside the wall, then knelt inconspicuously to where his hand could clutch onto and lift the crowbar from the dirt mound. Nick stood idle and watched.

"You're crazy! You don't know what you're talking about," James denied with boldness.

William's thought was to torture the lying thief until he confessed because he wasn't willing to walk out with his tail between his legs. He wanted proof and he wanted to see the money so he thrust himself forward and seized James by his arm.

James withdrew his free arm around to his backside and pulled a pistol out from the belt line of his pants. He tried to aim it at William amid the struggle.

"What are you gonna do – shoot all of us?" William thundered as he let go of his arm to try and grab hold of the arm that was attached to the gun.

"It's a warning for you to get out of here."

Both Saul and Nick ducked behind the boiler to protect themselves from flying bullets. Saul maneuvered himself to the other side of the large kettle, then hastened toward the criminal with the crowbar in midair ready to smack the gun from James' hand.

William lifted his knee and rammed it into James' back.

"Uuh!" he groaned.

Saul smacked the metal tool down on the pistol causing it to drop to the ground.

The agent spun James around and slammed him up against the boiler. "We could do this all night. It's up to you."

"Okay, okay. Calm down," James hollered, then gasped for air. "If you let me go now, I'll give you each ten grand. We all walk away and we never tell a sole."

"I'll go for that deal," Nick spoke up from behind the boiler.

"I knew I had the right guy!" William boasted as he put his hand to James' throat.

Nick cast his eyes downward at the hatch and observed it to be slightly open. He knelt and pointed his flashlight into the opening and saw a large white sackcloth bag. "Hey guys, look at this."

While William kept James restrained, Saul stepped to Nick and helped him pull the sack out into view.

The agents heard the sound of a click and cast their vision to the source.

"Freeze it right there." Linda Lolly stood in the doorway with a 9mm pointed directly at them. "And you -" she gestured to William with her weapon, "Let him go." She slurred her words as she spoke.

William sensed her drunken state as he watched her hold the gun with an unstable hand. Saul and Nick also kept an eye on the bank robbers while they slowly withdrew themselves from the boiler's hatch.

James advanced to the front of the metal tank and stooped down to grab the sackcloth bag. He stepped away and picked his pistol up off the ground, then joined his wife. "We'll keep them locked in the basement til we can rehide the money," he whispered to her as he kept his pistol aimed on the bounty hunters. "There's no proof it was us."

William and Saul glanced at each other with aggression in their faces just waiting for an opportunity.

Linda gyrated and tottered through the scant enclosure to the staircase. She ascended three steps, then stumbled. She fell against the wall, then backwards into James. Her 9mm dropped to the step from which she fell.

James broke Linda's fall, but the force knocked him on his ass. "What the hell Linda?" he roared as he tried to free his gun from the weight of her body.

The agents witnessed the pickled display of James and Linda and saw that the two weapons were down so they hastened in a furtive manner to the duo. They knew it was their chance to pounce and capture the thieves.

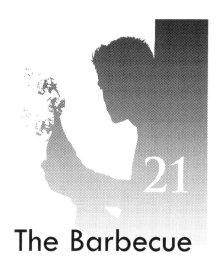

# The Barbecue

Dominique recalled the knock at her door as she lay on her bed thinking about the invite. She felt thrilled to be shown attention once again by a man since her divorce, however, she made herself to be more aware of what she wanted out of a new relationship. Before she agreed to go out with him, she told him she wanted a man who loved the Lord and didn't drink or do drugs. Saul claimed he was both.

"Mom?" Ian stepped through her open doorway into her bedroom. "When are you leaving?"

"Soon. And I won't be gone long."

He laid on his stomach next to her. "So is he your new boyfriend now?"

She smiled. "No. It's only his birthday and he wanted me to join him at his barbecue. He asked your brothers and William to go also."

"But not me?"

"You could go."

"I don't want to."

Nathan stayed at home with Ian. They decided they were going to spend their time tossing the football in their mother's indoor swimming pool.

Ian loved to jump from the edge and catch Nathan's throws in midair before dropping into the water.

After Nathan took his turn at catching the ball, he stepped out of the pool to smoke a cigarette. While he sat on a lounge chair, he heard a soft voice call out his name from above. He looked up. "Felica?" he whispered.

"It's me." She then showed herself.

"Hey girl. Where have you been the last couple of weeks?"

"With my parents."

"You're looking good."

She blushed only for a moment.

Nathan thought on how she left suddenly. "I don't want to be rude or insensitive, but why did you come here?"

"I left without saying good-bye."

"Yea – you just kind of faded away." He took a puff from his cigarette.

"I was told to leave." She glanced at Ian who was using the football to bob upon while he kicked his legs.

"He was having a bad day." Nathan answered quickly for his brother.

"That's okay Nathan. I'm over it." She descended from her floating position to the cement tiles and sat in the patio chair next to him. "I also wanted to set things right between us – about the getting married part."

Nathan became a bit apprehensive, hoping she wasn't going to press the issue of marriage. He watched her in awe with his large brown eyes because he still had a crush on her.

"I've done a lot of thinking about this and I don't expect you to marry me just because you kissed me. It was a silly idea."

"But you never know what can happen in the future." he added without thinking.

She grinned and her eyes began to glow.

There was a moment of silence. "You want to come swimming with us?"

Saul had his briquettes piled within his grill ready to douse with charcoal fluid and set afire to.

206

Dominique stepped out of her white Ford Explorer and headed across the yard toward Saul. She glanced at him as he stood by his two guests. She could see he was watching her too. She wore a smile on her face as she walked over the scant grassy trail. She felt nervous as she approached the three men; one she didn't recognize.

Saul's friend stood up. "I'll see you on another day Saul." He cast his eyes on Dominique. "Hi," he spoke to her, then left.

"See ya Lloyd," Saul called out.

Dominique stopped near Saul and waved a quick hello to William who was sitting in the lawn chair next to Lloyd's empty chair. She turned to Saul. "Why's your friend leaving?"

"He has to be in Moscow in a few hours."

"Hmm," she murmured, then looked at him with a smile. "So.. Happy Birthday."

"Thank you."

"You know you're only twenty days older than me." She made her comment due to information she learned from a previous conversation.

He was grinning back at her. "That still makes me the boss!" She laughed.

Saul lit a cigarette as he kept his focus on Dominique's facial features that included her immense blue eyes and her smooth rosy cheeks.

"I saw you two Sherlocks in the newspaper last week," she spoke, then sat on one of the lawn chairs.

"Yes, we are heroes," William asserted proudly.

"And we're still waiting to see if there's a cash reward."

"Whew-hew!" Dominique cheered as she raised her forearms twice in a quick motion. "That will be great for you guys."

"Yea," Saul answered, "I'd buy me a 4-wheeler." He observed his next guests to be arriving so he set fire to his briquettes.

Travis and Hannah exited their truck and walked slow upon the trodden down path that led to the barbecue site.

Dominique stood to her feet and as she stepped past Saul, she gave a little push to his arm.

"Hey!" he roared jokingly.

She advanced to greet her son and daughter-in-law. "How's the leg?" she asked Hannah.

"It's still sore, but I'm getting around better every day."

"That's good to hear." She turned her attention to Travis and waited for him to reveal his mother-in-law problem.

He observed her tacit expression and spoke. "Things are working out for us Mom."

"Yea?"

"Hannah's mom agreed to let her stay with me on the weekends and she'll stay at her mom's during the week so she can finish her senior year with her friends."

"That sounds like a good arrangement - for now."

Hannah nodded in agreement.

"There's more." He glanced at William and saw him to be preoccupied with talking to Saul. "I'm gonna give up being a bounty hunter and find a job over in Coeur d' Alene."

"And then move there?"

"Yes so we can be closer to each other." He wrapped his muscular arm around Hannah's waist and applied a light squeeze.

"What kind of work will you be looking for?"

"Well, Hannah's cousin works at a nursery and he said the owners will be looking to hire someone next week."

"Nursery as in trees, plants, rocks..?"

"Yes," Hannah answered with a giggle. "I can't see Travis taking care of a bunch of little kids."

"At least not yet, huh?" Dominique peeked over her right shoulder at Saul who was now creeping her way. She turned and stepped toward him while Travis and Hannah headed for the lawn chairs.

"Come help me." He gestured with a nod of his head for her to follow him. They advanced to the back door of his small stone house and after he opened the door for her, they entered in.

She stood in his kitchen where she watched him open the refrigerator door and withdraw a plate that contained a stack of raw hamburger patties. She noticed paper plates and chips and buns atop of the counter as well as a large grilling spatula. "You wear that hat all the time?" She was curious.

"Yes I do," he answered.

"Why? Don't you like the wind to blow in through your hair?"

He set the plate on the counter. "Cuz I'm bald."

"No you're not. Really?" She had never dated a bald man before. "Let me see?" She playfully reached her hand up to his head to grab his cap.

He quickly clutched onto her tiny wrist so she couldn't remove it. "For a kiss you can take it off."

She tried to pull and wriggle free from his tight grip, but it was useless. "You're hurting me." She became unamused.

He released her wrist. "Sorry, I guess I'm just too strong." He then removed his cap for her to see.

"You're only half bald," she spoke as she rubbed her sore wrist. "Now you know."

Nick and his girlfriend Jen appeared and stood at the back door. "Hey Mom," Nick greeted, "and Saul."

Saul moved his attention to them. "You two made it." His deep voice sounded throughout the kitchen. "Come help us carry stuff outside." He returned to the refrigerator for the cheese slices and store bought potato salad.

The couple advanced through the kitchen toward Saul while Dominique grabbed the paper plates and barbecue sauce and stepped out the back door. She retreated to the group and after she set the commodities on the cheap portable table, she sat in a lawn chair next to Travis. She was quiet as she secretly eyed the red marks on her wrist. She could still make out the imprints of his banana fingers.

Saul, Nick, and Jen came out of the house with the rest of the goods. Saul had his back to the crowd as he slapped the meat patties onto the hot grill.

Dominique watched him and began to wonder if it was a good idea for her to continue to see this rough and tough bounty hunter man. In a way it was a turn-on to her, however, she sensed God telling her no.

"Mom?" Travis bid for her attention. "Mom?"

"Huh?" She turned her head quickly to him. "I was lost in thought."

"I was just going to tell you I went to court yesterday."

"How did that go?"

"The judge reduced the charges to child endangerment. I got a small fine and one year supervised probation."

"Supervised?"

"Yea – It's retarded. And some of the lame stipulations for me," he added, "Is that I can't go near any elementary schools or any playgrounds."

"So basically where there's any kids?"

"Right," he replied, "And next month on Halloween, I can't even open my door and pass out candy to them."

"Wow.. They've made you out to be a pervert."

"I know. It sux, but at least I don't have to register as a sex offender." He took a cigarette out of his pack to smoke it.

"Thank God! That could ruin your career." She then glanced at Saul who was studying her with a sly eye.

Saul jerked his head back to express for her to join him at the grill. Jen was helping to arrange the edibles on the table while the rest of the party chatted with one another from their chairs. William listened to Nick as he talked of his race car.

Dominique stood and sauntered his way. The smell of barbecue wafted through the air. At the grill, she eyed the burgers. "Mmm – they're looking tasty."

He was wearing a grin. "I bought you something today."

She felt surprised. Her heart reacted in a playful manner to his affection. "Are you trying to woo me now?"

"Of course." He reached into his jeans pocket and pulled out a turquoise heart-shaped stone of about one inch by one inch and handed it to her.

"Ohh.. It's awesome. Thank you." She paused as she looked it over. "But it's your birthday. I should be giving you something." She cast a peek upon the curious mix of charm and mystery in his blue-green eyes.

"Well," he shot back, "You still owe me a kiss!"

# THE END!

Printed in the United States
By Bookmasters